BEEFSTEW SAVES LIVES ON D-DAY

A Young Flier Thinks Outside the Box to Dramatically Reduce Casualties at Normandy

WILLIAM C. GRAYSON

∞ INFINITY
PUBLISHING

ISBN: 978-1-4958-2146-2
eBook ISBN: 978-1-4958-2147-9
Library of Congress Control Number: 2018902499

Published March 2018

INFINITY PUBLISHING
1094 New DeHaven Street, Suite 100
West Conshohocken, PA 19428-2713
Toll-free (877) BUY BOOK
Local Phone (610) 941-9999
Fax (610) 941-9959
Info@buybooksontheweb.com
www.buybooksontheweb.com

Also by William C. Grayson

- *Delaware's Ghost Towers, The Coast Artillery's Forgotten Last Stand During the Darkest Days of World War II,* 1st and 2nd Editions, ISBN 978-0-7414-4906-4
- *At Least I Know I'm Free, How Americans Could Have Lost Their Freedoms,* ISBN 0-7414-4036-9
- *Chicksands: A Millennium of History,* 1st, 2nd, and 3rd Editions, ISBN 0-9633208-1-5
- *Ear on the War in Vietnam* and *Presidential Visit, both* included in the book, *These Guys,* Old Lt. Press
- *Chicksands: The Battle of Britain and the Blitz,* Shefford Press
- Article: *WWII Museums – Fort Miles, Delaware,* published in *Military Magazine*
- Two Book Reviews: *The Price of Vigilance* and *Secret War,* published in *Military Magazine*
- A Double Book Review: *Scorpion Down* and *All Hands Down* in *The Phoenician* (Journal of NSA retirees)
- Article: *China, Iran and North Korea Filling Vacuums,* published in *Military Magazine*
- Two Chapters: *Headquarters Closure and Filling Sandbags* published by McManmon Associates in *New Ideas in Management*
- Textbook: *Introduction to Communications Security,* Computer Security Institute
- Textbook: *Securing Computer Centers,* MIS Training Institute

Neal Taylor, the National Spin-Casting Champion, recalls fishing with President Eisenhower in 1960, when the President suddenly stopped fishing and sat down with a troubled expression. Taylor asked if he was feeling all right.

Ike replied, "Not a day goes by that I don't think about the many men, who lost their lives at Normandy." [*http:// flyfishingwithjeff.com*].

WHY?

WHY NORMANDY?

DEDICATION

The Operation OVERLORD invasion of Normandy was an indispensable component of saving the western way of life and its precious freedoms for successive generations. Hundreds of thousands of Allied men and women played important roles in the operation's many phases and a great many sacrificed much. 4414 Allied soldiers were killed storming the Normandy beaches. Sadly, none knew that their side won. They died for us and this book is gratefully dedicated to them.

FOREWORD AND ACKNOWLEDGEMENTS

So much was going on all at once in Europe during World War II that it requires careful concentration to parse the war's many major decisions, events, and blunders in order to compile a prioritized list of those most important. I propose these three as the most important in the European Theater:

- June 1940 – the rescue of over 330,000 British and Allied troops from Dunkirk. German capture of those men in France would have likely led to Britain's withdrawal from the war with terrible consequences for the British and, shortly after, for Americans.
- Summer of 1940 – fighting and winning the Battle of Britain instead of suing for peace with Hitler in hopes of getting the best terms possible. Anything short of victory against the *Luftwaffe* would have made the United Kingdom unavailable from which to bomb German forces and industry and, later, to launch an invasion of occupied Europe.
- June 6, 1944 – the successful Allied landings on the Normandy beaches.

Prime Minister Winston Churchill told the House of Commons on June the 6th

*"This vast operation is undoubtedly the most complicated
and difficult that has ever occurred. It involves tides, wind,
waves, visibility, both from the air and the sea standpoint,
and the combined employment of land, air and sea forces in
the highest degree of intimacy and in contact with conditions
which could not and cannot be fully foreseen."*

In recognition of the unmatched importance of the
Normandy invasion, historians, novelists, and film-
makers have not and probably never will stop trying
to describe and explain it from different perspectives.
Even among writers of Alternative History, the subject
is irresistible, although a high percentage of that genre
focuses on how life would be different, if Hitler had won.

Most of us – myself included – knew only the basics
about "D-Day" and received some education from
watching the film, *The Longest Day* (20th Century
Fox/1962). Personally, I can't recall how many times I
have watched that film, enough though to play several
parts in three languages. Actor Rod Steiger, playing a
Destroyer Skipper on the evening of June 5th suggests,
"We are on the eve of a day that people are going to
talk about long after we are dead and gone." The film's
scriptwriter was certainly prescient 56 years before this
writing.

In 1998, Dreamworks and Paramount Pictures released
Saving Private Ryan. Steven Spielberg makes sure the
viewer fully understands what the troops in the first
wave ashore faced in the form of ready-and-waiting
German defenders with the world's fastest-firing
machine guns and mortars as they tried to cross a beach
studded with landmines. The gruesome detail – in color

- far surpasses that of *The Longest Day* made in black and white 36 years earlier.

But a question in my mind that never went away asked why casualties were so high – especially at Omaha Beach – after so many bombers dropped thousands of high explosive bombs along the beaches in the wee hours of June 6th and the largest naval armada in history with the biggest guns ever afloat pounded the German defensive emplacements as soon as it was light enough to see.

Sixteen years after the Normandy landings, Dwight Eisenhower was still troubled specifically about Normandy, even though other World War II engagements resulted in higher casualty numbers.

From The Daily Telegraph (UK):

The US National D-Day Memorial Foundation has verified a total of 4414 dead in Normandy on June 6, 1944:

- 2499 Americans
- 1915 from the other Allied nations *(http://www. telegraph.co.uk/news/2016/06/06/d-day-landings-operation-overlord-in-numbers2)*

However -

- In the push to the Rhine River, the US Army suffered over 50,000 killed, over 172,000 wounded, and many missing.
- Over 75,000 Americans died during the Battle of the Bulge.
- Over 52,000 members of the US Army Air Forces in Europe were killed in action.

Why was Normandy so troubling to Ike? Did he believe more could have been done to save lives?

At my core, I am an Intelligence Analyst with many years involved in tactical air operations and analyzing various foreign air forces. Over time, I came to wonder why the Allies, with thousands of combat aircraft in England and almost total air superiority in the skies of France, didn't provide continuous, low-level, Close Air Support for the troops as they were hitting the beaches. I think the answer is simple: ***nobody thought of it***.

For years, I pondered that question on-and-off until I watched *Saving Private Ryan* for the second time in early 2017. Then, I started analyzing the problem.

Churchill called the Normandy invasion "*. . . the most complicated and difficult that has ever occurred.*"[1] As soon as I started thinking about scheduling the times over target for a large number of aircraft flying low where big naval guns were supposed to have stopped firing and where swarms of infantry would be jumping out of landing craft, complexity and difficulty surfaced immediately. It became clear that Command and Control (C2) of the air assets would have been essential but that in 1944, no such C2 capabilities were available. Very limited Tactical Air C2 came from a flight leader, fully engaged in the mission, doing with his airplane what all his men were doing with theirs.

Pilots would have needed daylight to see camouflaged emplacements on the ground and would have had to fly from east to west so the rising sun was behind

---

[1] Speaking to Parliament on June 6, 1944.

them. Starting the low-level attack from the much safer Atlantic Ocean - from west to east - with the early rising sun in their own eyes and behind German defenders' eyes would not have worked. And large, high explosive bombs dropped from aircraft on targets at the edge of a beach approximately a quarter-mile wide as troops were coming ashore from landing craft would have been dangerously impractical.

The targets of the naval guns and the objectives of the landing troops depended on accurate, up-to-date intelligence that was hard to come by. *The Longest Day* film factually tells the story of the 2nd and 5th Ranger Battalions, who climbed the cliffs at the *Pointe du Hoc* only to discover that the big guns they were sent to destroy had been moved. The available intelligence didn't include that.

Allied headquarters in London depended on the French *Résistance* for a lot of the specific, detailed intelligence on German capabilities in Normandy. In an era when so many of us use "social media" all day long, can't walk in public without looking at a phone, and spend much of our waking hours in contact with *someone,* it was instructive to imagine how utterly unreliable, difficult and slow were the means of communication during World War II. This was especially true in France under watchful, brutal German occupation.

So, I have invented situations, characters, dialogues, and actions I believe to be plausible. I hope my readers agree.

Historical Fiction vs Alternative History: the Difference

- In Historical Fiction, the **actual events are <u>unchanged</u>** but the characters (some real/some imagined) say and do things that, perhaps, didn't happen.
- In Alternative History, the characters (some real/some imagined) say and do things that, perhaps didn't happen and **the events described are <u>imagined.</u>**

Acknowledgements

Much valuable assistance was provided by friends and family, who listened to and questioned my alternate concept for the Normandy landings and critiqued the manuscript. History Professor Gary Wray made valuable suggestions about German weaponry. Major General Gary O'Shaughnessy (USAF Ret.), Brigadier Chris Holtom, (British Army, Ret.), Historian Mike Morgan, Colonel Vic Brown (USAF Ret.) and Don Kline reviewed my historical assertions and the plausibility of my fictional inserts. All four also helped me organize the story's complex timeline across three generations. Major Gina Jones (USMC Ret) and Tessa Sherman, both aviatrices, checked the book's flying content for plausibility. Dr. Elliott Klonsky, OD checked me on the main character's detached retina and my brother, Dr. George Grayson, MD kept me straight on the relationship between Yellow Fever and liver disease and European geography. My son John calculated the math for spacing the D-Day aircraft. My daughter Amy, son James, and grandson Reese. Cindy Loesch and Ed Fellini critiqued the story line and alerted me to needed editorial fixes. The aforementioned Gina Jones and Tom Kramer helped me find many of the photos embedded in the text. The staff at the Fort Meade

Museum was especially supportive in helping me locate World War I artifacts and arranging exhibits so that I could photograph them.

Photo Credits

Individual photo credits are included in the end notes for each chapter. Every effort has been made to trace copyright holders of photos annotated by the Photographs and Prints Division of the Library of Congress "no known restrictions." If advised, the publisher will rectify any omissions at the earliest opportunity.

TABLE OF CONTENTS

Chapter		Page

CHAPTER 1

1943 in England - Stu Rittersberg

Army Air Forces First Lieutenant Stu Rittersberg put both hands to his head massaging his left temple and made a prolonged "*mmmmm*" sound.

"That bump on the head still bothering you?" asked his office mate, RAF Flying Officer[2] Reg Childs from across their shared work table.

"Yeah, just won't completely go away."

"Let's go outside for some air," Reg suggested. We've been on this problem for four hours straight.

"No, I'll be OK in a minute." Stu gripped the table edge with both hands and raised his chin toward the ceiling and stretched. Once again, the elusive memory gap came uninvited to the front of his mind to taunt him and he tried to break its opaque shell.

He remembered the mission easily – much of it in slow motion detail - even though some scenes exceeded 400 knots. His memory was sharp about his two German Bf109 kills and the definite damage his guns did to a third.

---

[2] Equivalent to US First Lieutenant

And he could still feel the banging hits on the underside of his P-38 that came from nowhere, clearly remembered the resulting vibration and his instinctive thought processes assessing his situation.

P-38 "Lightning"

He wasn't wounded, his plane was still flyable and responsive to his stick and rudder and throttle changes. No smoke, no fire and the note of his two Allison engines was normal.

But when he looked around, he was no longer in the swirling dogfight; not a plane in sight. He began a wide left turn while looking for the rest of his flight when he recognized his lead's voice in his headphones, "Beechnut Flight: Let's head for home. Beefstew – where are you?"

Stu remembered answering, changing course for his base, RAF Westhampnett, finally catching up with the other returning P-38s, merging into the landing, pattern, lowering his landing gear, routinely descending to the runway, slowing to an Indicated Airspeed of 100 knots and feeling the wheels firmly contact the runway. That was all he could retrieve, however many times he searched his brain.

Following the vexing gap, Stu's next memory was in the base dispensary's Operating Room. The left side of his head was throbbing and his vision was blurred by what seemed to be a storm of black ants floating in front of him. Anesthesia was applied and Stu came awake in a base dispensary bed. What he couldn't remember was the left landing gear of his P-38 collapsing as soon as it touched the concrete, causing the plane to begin a violent cartwheel off the runway and very abruptly stopping upside down. Stu's head was slammed hard against the canopy's metal frame. His leather flying cap provided no protection and his raised goggles were hammered against his temple, all resulting in major bruising from his left ear to his eye socket and left cheek. He also suffered a detached retina in his left eye, causing bothersome "floaters" and the blurred, distorted vision that would end his days as a pilot.

That unhappy news came from a doctor at the US Army General Hospital at Bath, where Stu had been transferred. The doctor told Stu that he had been very lucky to survive the crash and had tried to be reassuring by predicting that Stu would walk out of the hospital with no physical disabilities. He added; however, that the Staff Flight Surgeon had already decertified Stu from flying and that the paperwork was being prepared to evacuate him back to the US for continuing observation of his detached retina.

P-39 "Airacobra"

As were his father and grandfather before him, Stu was a graduate of the US Military Academy at West Point, in the Class of 1940 and military service was in his genes. Despite what was intended as helpful career guidance from his father, Colonel Franz Steuben Rittersberg, Jr., Stu followed a dream to fly and - upon graduation from West Point - entered Undergraduate Pilot Training at Randolph Field in Texas. After winning his wings and completing advanced training, 2nd Lieutenant Stu Rittersberg was assigned to the 31st Pursuit Group at Selfridge Field Michigan, flying the P-39 Bell Airacobra. Stu immediately fell in love with his P-39's power and maneuverability.

The pilots of the 31st were a close-knit, cocky bunch, much like a college fraternity. All were about the same age, top-notch physical specimens with acute vision, balance, and reflexes. They all shared a love of flying and sense of being "special." Much of their free time on the ground was spent in discussing flying and telling flying stories flavored by good-natured banter spiced by barbed teasing. Everyone had a nickname: Gene Kowalski became "Ski," Ken Budelman became "Bud," Gerry Webb became "Spider," and Stu Rittersberg's "Beefstew." fit right in.

Right after the Japanese attack on Pearl Harbor, the unit was redesignated the 31st Fighter Group and alerted for deployment to England. Prior to shipping out, however, the Air Corps determined the P-39 unsuitable for long-distance formation ferry flights so the Group crossed the Atlantic by ship and arrived at their new station without their aircraft. Stu was upset at leaving his beloved *Airacobra* behind but soon forgot her as he began transitioning to the hotter twin-engine P-38 *Lightning*.

The 31st practiced aerial combat tactics and low-level strafing over gunnery ranges in Scotland, becoming fully operational in August 1942. Stu flew two uneventful missions in support of the British/Canadian raid on Dieppe followed by months of escorting coastal reconnaissance patrols during which he never saw an enemy aircraft. Finally, on a mission escorting B-17s in 1943, which saw the Group over northern France, Stu logged his two kills and sustained damage himself.

In his hospital bed, Stu was deeply dispirited by the news of his grounding and his uncertain future. Would all his boyhood fascination with white puffy clouds and curiosity about flying amongst them and the compelling image of the first airplane he ever saw now come to nothing? His father was his only family and he was somewhere in North Africa. Stu had no home to return to, no roots anywhere, no preparation for a career. He agonized about being medically discharged and having to look for some civilian job when there was so much to be done to defeat his country's enemies.

A spoken "Thank you" in a familiar voice woke Stu from having dozed off. It was his father, standing at his bedside with a concerned expression.

"Hi Pop. What are you doing here? I thought you were in Africa."

"I was but Ike wants me at ETOUSA[3] in London, watching over what he got started in June. I only got to England yesterday and came right over to check on you. How're you doing Son," his father asked.

They chatted about his mission, the crash, and his injuries until Stu brought up his grounding and what would now become of him. Stu made it clear to his father, now wearing the star of a Brigadier General, that he had nothing and no one to go home to, now that Grandpa was gone. He needed to stay in the Army and wanted to stay in England to make a difference. He also thought he owed a debt to France that must be repaid.

---

[3] ETOUSA: European Theater of Operations, US Army

"Can't promise you anything just now but I'll see what I can do. In the meantime, concentrate on getting better and think positive thoughts," the General suggested. He squeezed Stu's shoulder, said "See you in a couple of days," gave him an encouraging smile, and walked off.

CHAPTER 2

Young Franz Steuben Rittersberg, Jr. (Stu's Father)

F ranz Jr. (known to all as "Frank") was as close to Dwight Eisenhower as a brother would have been. In 1912, both were on the West Point football team and were roommates when the Army team travelled to away games. Frank had grown up near Harrisburg, Pennsylvania and was a star athlete at the Harrisburg Academy prep school. He and Jim Thorpe had known each other as friendly rivals when Frank's team played Thorpe's school in football or ran track

Jim Thorpe

against them. Thorpe was already recognized as a future champion athlete, and, at the Army-Carlyle Indian School football game on November 9th, Frank brought Thorpe and Ike together for a friendly handshake.

It was during that game that Ike tackled the fleet-footed Thorpe and then hobbled to the sideline. Ike had suffered a knee injury that forever ended his football days. Frank felt Ike's injury as though it was his own. Ike stayed with the football team as a coach's assistant and remained close to Frank right through graduation with the West Point Class of 1915.

As cadets, both were fascinated by Winston Churchill's call for a "land battleship" to be used against the German lines in France. Churchill, then First Sea Lord[4], had been following studies and trials of what would become Britain's first tanks. Cadets Eisenhower and Rittersberg often conversed well into the night, enthusiastically dreaming of getting in on the ground floor of what they both saw as a natural progression from traditional horse cavalry.

Following graduation and commissioning as Army Second Lieutenants, both young officers entered on active duty in an Army that wasn't yet being prepared for war in France. But as the years passed into 1916 and 1917, the likelihood of a US entry into the war was increasing.

---

[4] Equivalent to US Secretary of the Navy.

CHAPTER 3

June 1917 - Seeing Franz Jr, off to France

Franz Sr. (Stu's grandfather) was one of the few who knew what was really going on in France during the early years of World War I. He was privy to a great deal of information that was withheld from the American people as public opinion began swinging in favor of US intervention. Many Americans were furious with Germany over the Lusitania sinking, the massive sabotage explosion at the "Black Tom" docks in New York harbor, and the perfidious *"Zimmerman Telegram."* Many felt that "enough was enough." Franz Sr. also knew the unpublished casualty statistics, knew about the effects of poison gas on the battlefield, knew that France and Britain were near exhaustion in available manpower, money, and innovative tactics that could break the trench warfare stalemate.

Franz Sr. was conflicted about his son, Frank, going into the meatgrinder that was eastern France. A West Pointer himself and recently-retired Army colonel, he was bursting with pride that Frank had followed in his footsteps but became suddenly unnerved when he received the news that Frank's unit, the US First Army, had been ordered to sail "over there" with General Pershing.

He put on his Army uniform for the first time in two years and took the train from Harrisburg to New York and then to the pier by taxi. Frank was hard to spot in the large crowd of Doughboys, all similarly attired but he did and got his attention by waving his uniform cap. Frank came over and saluted his father as they stood face-to-face. Frank looked fit in his Captain's uniform and had a confident smile.

For all his adult life, Franz Sr. had stolidly kept his emotions in check. Although deeply grieving when Frank's mother died and a year later, when Frank's little sister also died, the old soldier outwardly maintained his composure. But when he returned the respectful salute from this young man dressed for a war he knew to be terrible, his throat constricted and his lower lip trembled. As he felt his eyes filling,

How Frank would have looked

he impulsively wrapped both arms around Frank in a tight hug he had never before given his adult son and buried his face against his collar. He sensed hearing the hinges creak on the box in which he had stored a lifetime of hidden emotions. No one could see or hear the father's sobs but, his own arms also hugging his father, Frank could feel the rhythmic heaves with his own chest.

CHAPTER 4

In France - September 12, 1918

C aptain Frank Rittersberg Jr. (Stu's father) was eager finally to be going into combat with his tank unit. After drilling for months, with the Renault tanks provided by France, the Americans, under the command of Lt. Colonel George Patton, were deemed ready and ordered into the field to help break a German strongpoint at St. Mihiel.

Consistently difficult and unreliable, the Renaults could make only 4 miles per hour and needed to come to a standstill before turning. Worse, they were notoriously prone to getting hung-up on large obstacles or, more often, stuck in deep mud. But they were impenetrable by rifle

Renault Tank

and machine gun fire and seemed the desperately-needed solution to the wearying trench warfare stalemate.

Patton's infectious enthusiasm for tanks as the future of battlefield dominance strongly affected Frank, who was proud to be in on the ground floor of the US Army Tank Corps.

Almost immediately after the unit came out of the treeline onto open ground at St. Mihiel, German 77mm/FK16 artillery rounds began raining down on five slow-crawling tanks led by Frank. Three of the tanks took direct hits, knocking them out of action, while several others lost forward progress despite uselessly grinding away with their tracks. Frank ordered his tank driver to get close to one of those with a track blown off and grey smoke seeping from the turret hatch. Revolver in hand, he leapt to the ground and was moving in a crouch to the disabled Renault when an exploding German round blew him off his feet and slammed him backward into his own tank. Sergeant Alton saw him writhing on the ground and, with the help of another tanker, hauled him back inside. After another nearby blast rendered their own 37mm gun inoperable, Sergeant Alton made the decision to get the Captain to an aid station so they slowly retreated back to the treeline.

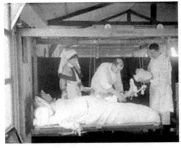
Frank was in and out of excruciating consciousness for 48 hours. When fully awake, he found his left leg in traction and immobilized by heavy wood splints. He had suffered three cracked ribs, a separated shoulder, and broken collarbone. His doctors weren't sure his separated knee could be satisfactorily reassembled to permit a normal walking pace. There were large, thick bandages on the left side of his neck and left forearm covering shrapnel wounds that had been cleaned and stitched.

Frank's first thoughts were about the fortunes of his tank crews but his questions were answered with reassuring generalities sparing him discouraging news that could wait.

When it was thought safe to move him, Frank endured a bumpy ambulance ride to Number 1 Field Hospital in the former *Hôtel Place* at Etretat, just up the Channel coast from the port city of Le Havre. A note in his hospital admission record marked him for convalescence until sufficiently mobile to handle a crossing by ship back to the US.

Uncomfortable, unhappy, and confused about his future, Frank sensed a powerful urge to regain control of his personal situation and to give directions about his care. He was mentally prepared to issue orders to the first hospital staff member, who showed up, but his attention was diverted to the arrival in the bed next to his by a grumpy guy, himself giving non-stop orders and directions. When his ward neighbor was finally tucked in and no longer surrounded by nurses and aides, Frank saw that it was his commander, Lt. Colonel George Patton, who had been shot through his left leg. Patton noticed Frank at the same time, excitedly exclaiming, "Frank! So good to see you made it. We were all pretty worried about you. You going to be OK?"

Their enthusiastic review of the battle and performance of the Renault tanks was interrupted by the arrival of a pretty French nurse carrying a bowl of water and washcloth. Frank already knew *Infirmière* [5] Marguerite Renier, who had arrived to change the dressings covering his neck and arm wounds. Before starting on Frank, she introduced herself to Patton as "*Soeur* [6] Maggi" and, having been answered in

---

[5] *Infirmière = Nurse*

[6] Sister

Patton's fluent French, told him in French, to let her know if he needed anything.

"Take special care of my comrade, Captain Rittersberg, there," he instructed her soberly. "He's a genuine hero, getting out of his tank to help his men. We have recommended him for a medal."

Maggi sat on the edge of Frank's bed and gave him the usual warm smile and penetrating gaze that drew him to her at their first meeting. She made him happy by just being there. He wasn't used to pretty girls smiling at him and peering so deeply into his eyes. Her touch was comforting and when she gently squeezed his arm, he felt assured. Frank began looking forward to her daily visits and

How Maggi would have looked in 1918

missed her on her day off, wondering what she might be doing. He enjoyed watching her move.

More than once, Frank noticed blood stains on Maggi's grey chambray uniform skirt and Maggi wasn't good at hiding her distress after the death of one of her patients. It was obvious that the ghastly, dirty wounds that arrived daily from the battlefields deeply affected her. On many evenings, Maggi was clearly exhausted from very long hours of ceaseless hurrying and multi-tasking, often with disappointing outcomes. She usually cheered up soon after arriving at his bed but he could tell when she had recently wiped away tears. Frank wished he could comfort her by putting his arms around her.

George Patton's wound was uncomplicated and he was discharged on crutches after only a week. He had been promoted to full Colonel, while in the hospital. Wishing Frank a speedy recovery, Patton's farewell acknowledged Frank's expressed intention to stay in the Army and in the Tank Corps. "When you are ready for a new assignment, be sure to let me know. I'll always have a spot for you." Patton gave Maggi a thankful "*Au revoir*" in his fluent French, including a repeat of his "special care" for Frank that summoned a warm smile. When Maggi was out of earshot, Patton observed, "Frank, I think Maggi's sweet on you!"

Later that day, Frank had an unexpected visitor. He introduced himself as "Senator Jim Davis of Pennsylvania." "I'm in France as chairman of the Loyal Order of Moose War Relief Commission and I promised your father I'd look in on you in the hospital." It was a pleasant visit and Davis took the opportunity to call out to the whole ward, asking for a show of hands, "Who hails from Pennsylvania?"

Senator James Davis

CHAPTER 5

Marguerite (Maggi) Renier

The war had cost Maggi dearly. Her father, a dockworker and French Army Reserve Corporal in the port city of Le Havre, was among the first to be mobilized in 1914 and went missing in the war's first clash at the Battle of the Marne. Actually *Caporal* Renier and two soldiers from his squad were hit directly while crossing No-Man's Land by two German artillery shells exploding milliseconds apart. Nothing of his remains were recovered, hence his "missing" status. Maggi's mother, Paulette, was devastated by unceasing hopeful anxiety. Her meager widow's pension did not cover her already frugal lifestyle. With no marketable work experience, Paulette fell immediately on hard times. But with so many men then in the army, women found it necessary to work and provide for their families. Paulette went to work in her cousin's bakery, a short walk down *La Rue Lavoisier* from home. At least Paulette had kitchen skills to offer and the bakery provided a small salary and much needed bread for her table.

Maggi's older brother, Jean and her fiancé, Henri, were conscripted together by the Army in 1915 and Maggi saw them both off at the train station. Her brother had introduced his best school chum, Henri, to her and was overjoyed at their subsequent engagement. It was a difficult decision in which Maggi's mother and brother had their say but the wedding plans were postponed until Henri's return.

It was Henri's blue eyes and deep-in-thought expression that had first captivated Maggi. Gazing deeply into what she felt was his soul, Maggi longed for his touch and kiss and was happiest when they were alone, together. Before Henri boarded the train, and their last desperate hug on the station platform, Maggi asked, "Will you come back?"

"Yes," Henri replied. His blue eyes brimming with tears, he asked Maggi to wait for him.

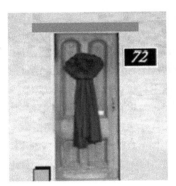

Maggi and her mother were nervously aware, passing so many neighbors' front doors along *Rue de Molière*, hung with black crepe, mourning sons and fathers. They were gripped with paralyzing apprehension by the letter-carrier's daily approach. The first news came in a letter from Jean. Henri had been wounded but Jean helped to get him in an ambulance and thought he would be all right. No description of the kind of wound or hint of where they were fighting filled both women with new questions but they clung to hope. Hope was dashed two weeks later when official word arrived that Henri had died in hospital some days earlier.

Distraught and wailing mournfully, Maggi was gathered into Paulette's arms, both women loudly moaning and sobbing. Her thoughts of her husband, Maggi's Henri, and all their neighbors were overwhelming.

"What is this terrible war for? What good will come of it?" For the Renier women, none. Maggi's brother, Jean, was killed three months later, joining the 1.3 million of his countrymen, who would die on French battlefields. Both Maggi and her mother slumped into deep depression, recognized by neighbors when they ventured outdoors as haggard, downcast and unsmiling. A compassionate neighbor, wearing the armband of the *Croix Rouge Français*[7] suggested to Paulette in the bakery that it would be good for Marguerite to get out of the house, begin a routine, and be with other people. If Marguerite was interested, she would help find her a place at the Field Hospital in nearby Etretat. With her mother's encouragement, Maggi went with their neighbor, Danielle, and found herself enthusiastically welcomed.

With only the briefest orientation, Maggi acquired the title *"Infirmière."*[8] At first, her duties only involved bed-making, cleaning and fetching but she was soon helping to care for patients and assisting doctors and the more senior nurses, who taught her how to deal with wounds.

Being busy and feeling useful changed Maggi's outlook, and for a while, she looked forward to the start of her work shift. But even without ever hearing the overwhelming roar of battle or experiencing a soldier's gripping fear before exposing himself to enemy fire or living through the horror of realizing oneself to have been seriously wounded, Maggi began to empathize deeply with her

[7] French Red Cross
[8] *Infirmière: Nurse*

patients. She fretted about how those with lost limbs or eyesight would fare when they went home. Those who had breathing difficulties after having been gassed filled her with sadness at the prospect that they would suffer for the rest of their lives. It was frustrating that she could not do more to help them.

Maggi yearned for the war to end and stop turning young men in perfect health to dreadfully disabled survivors so much in need of care. She found herself fantasizing about a normal life with a husband and her own children, somewhere quiet and far removed from the sadness she was witnessing daily.

Then there came Captain Franz Rittersberg, seriously wounded in the neck and in great pain from broken ribs and a dislocated knee. Upon hearing his name, Maggi warily assumed he must be a captured German officer but was delighted to learn that he was an American. Although his injuries would need care and time to heal, his face was unmarked and his sparkling blue eyes immediately reminded her of Henri. For his part, he was captivated by Maggi's smile. Girls usually didn't smile at him with such warmth.

As his pains subsided, Maggi found Frank easygoing and talkative but eager to get back on his feet. She was curious about his name so he explained. "I'm from the Pennsylvania Dutch country in America and my family has lived on the same farm there since the late 17th century. My father's name was "Franz" and I was named after him as "Franz junior." At first, I was called "Junior" but didn't like that so we settled on "Frank" because my father was already "Franz.""

He skipped the part about his ancestor, Christoph Rittersberg's dowry bargain with his good friend and neighbor, Otto Steuben, on the betrothal of his oldest son Heinricus to Elise Gertrudis Steuben in 1737. Otto confided in his friend that, with only one daughter to survive him, he was disappointed that his own family name would not be continued when he was gone. Without making it a condition of the marriage contract, Otto merely wished aloud that a grandson might be given the middle name "Steuben." That charming anecdote was kept alive to be told and retold and successive Rittersberg generations gave at least one baby boy the Steuben middle name in respect for their common colonial forebears.[9] On Otto's death, his farm adjoining Christoph's, was bequeathed to Elise, making the conjoined farms one of the largest properties in Dauphin County.

Maggi told Frank about the combat deaths of her father her brother, her brother's friends and that her mother was now working in a bakery. She didn't tell Frank that she had a fiancé, who was also killed in action. With brimming eyes, Maggi confessed that most of her family were gone as were her friends. "Except for my mother, I sometimes feel so alone."

As time passed, Frank continued to recover and it was Maggi, who helped him to stand and take his first steps in the room and then in the hospital hallway. Maggi and Frank came to recognize the easy rapport between them and both, independently, allowed the thought that there might be a future together. A frequent subject of

---

[9] Frank couldn't have known in 1919 that his own great-grandson would adopt the hyphenated surname Steuben-Rittersberg. Otto would have been pleased!

their conversations was "Pennsylvania." Frank enjoyed providing glowing descriptions, daring to think that Maggi might want to go home with him. Her prolonged, penetrating eye contact encouraged Frank, who had for a while been seeing her as Maggi the girl as opposed to Maggi the nurse. For the first time in his life, he felt a compelling desire to be alone with a girl and to touch her.

CHAPTER 6

Christmas 1918 - Etretat Hospital

Frank had been up and walking unaided except for a cane and enjoyed getting out in the cold air. Maggi encouraged him to go further each day and, when she could, walked with him in town among the old half-timbered buildings along *Rue Monge* or along the waterfront Promenade. Sometimes she held his hand. Frank confessed that he was wary of leaving the hospital

Hôtel Place – the US hospital

grounds and walking to the Channel shore in case he stumbled on uneven ground and fell.

The French Government provided a Christmas Dinner at the hospital, celebrating the end of "The Great War." Maggi and Frank sat together, looking more at each other than at what was on their dinner plates. They both drank some champagne and exchanged toasts to peace and a happy future. With a some trepidation, Frank gave Maggi a little gift-wrapped bottle of *Brise de Violettes* perfume. Obviously excited, she opened it right away, was impressed by his choice, and reached across to touch Frank's hand. She rubbed a few drops on her left wrist and held it out for him to smell. The moment found them in a shared, encouraging smile.

At that festive party, Maggi was genuinely relieved that there would be no more wounded and maimed young men arriving by ambulance. Part of her job at the hospital had been meeting the daily convoy of ambulances that brought wounded men from "hospital trains" at the station. She had attended so many in their last moments of life, distraught that she could not help them. She was relieved now to have that behind her.

After dinner, Maggi suggested getting some fresh air and guided Frank slowly down the Promenade steps and through the dune grass out to the edge of the white chalk cliffs,[10] where they stood silently, enjoying the tang of the cold salt air and rhythmic lapping of the surf. It was a clear night; the sky was full of stars. Standing closely together side-by-side, Maggi reached across her body with her right hand, gripped Frank's right arm and rested her head on his shoulder. She had put some of the perfume behind her ears. Frank thought she smelled gorgeous.

Grateful that the war was finally over and happy with Christmas spirit, Maggi permitted herself the wish that perhaps she might have a future with Frank. It was the first time she had gone further than holding his hand and hoped he would give some positive sign of romantic interest.

---

[10] The white chalk cliffs at Etretat resemble those across the English Channel at Dover.

"I love the bouquet of the salt water," Maggi said. "It is the aroma I most associate with home."

"Do you think you could be happy in a place far from the ocean? A place with many trees and big farms and friendly, gentle people?"

"Perhaps."

Aware of his obvious but as yet unspoken affection, she wanted him to kiss her and she was ready. Frank turned to her, put a hand on the back of her neck and pulled her toward his face. The kiss was soft and brief but, after a few moments, followed by another and several more, full of expressed desire and mutual acceptance. As one, they knelt briefly until Maggi was lying back in the tall grass. Frank joined her and the hungry kissing resumed.

Fully aware that there had been nothing of passion in her life since her 1915 farewell with Henri, Maggi yielded willingly to the mounting sensations of desire and pleasure, lightly holding his head, returning Frank's kisses as acceptance of his lead. His urgent touches and, very quickly, his hand inside her clothing excited her to a dreaminess she hadn't felt since Henri and she unconsciously made soft murmuring sounds. But Frank continued well past the point at which Henri had always stopped, signaling silently that anything further must wait until the wedding. Confused but still in tingling ecstasy, Maggi sensed the encounter proceeding unbidden by either of them. She was confused by his movements and a momentary sharp pain followed soon after by Frank, now by her side, breathing heavily.

Putting his arm across her, Frank was about to blurt, "I love you" when a bewildered Maggi, back to reality, stiffened and got to her feet. Straightening her clothes, she stammered, "I must go" and walked quickly toward the stairs to the Promenade, feeling angry, guilty and ashamed at the same time.

Fumbling for his cane and then back on his feet, Frank followed as fast as he could in the direction she went. He looked everywhere for her in and around the hospital but she was gone. Later, alone in his hospital bed, anguished guilt kept him awake until almost dawn.

His brief sleep was cut short by staff bustling in the hospital room, opening shutters and clinking glass and metal objects. Unsure of what to say in the apology he knew was due, Frank waited for Maggi to come and change the dressings on his wounds but, instead, Sister Beryl, a British nurse he had seen before in the ward, approached, wished him a cheery "Good Morning" and started changing the dressings.

"Where is Sister Maggi?" he asked, trying to conceal his anxiety.

"Don't know love, she 'asn't come in yet."

Frank waited anxiously for Maggi all that day and the next. Maggi didn't show and no one had any answers for him concerning her whereabouts. When he finally learned where she had roomed in Etretat, near the hospital, further inquiries led him only to the sorrowing news that she had gone suddenly on her bicycle without leaving a forwarding address. No one told Frank that Maggi might have gone home to Le Havre.

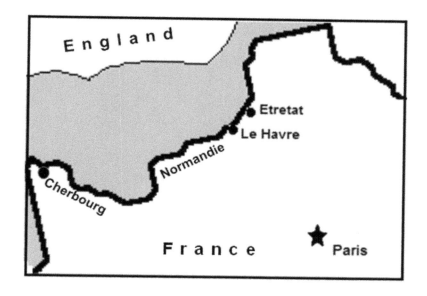

CHAPTER 7

December 1918 - Maggi: Back in Le Havre

Overwrought with feelings of guilt and shame, Maggi left Etretat and pedaled to her mother's house on the *Rue de Molière*. Madame Renier was happy but concerned to see Maggi, who explained she had always intended to work at the hospital until she was no longer needed. That day had now come and she felt her place was at home, helping her mother. Maggi's face and body language weren't convincing but her mother didn't press her. Whatever her daughter wanted to confide in her mother would come later.

Maggi's own insomnia produced a self-promise to go to church and confession, which she did the next day. *Père* Antoine[11] was in his 70s and had known Maggi all her life. He had been called back to the parish out of retirement because so many younger priests had accompanied local units to the front as chaplains. Immediately suspicious that he was about to hear another of the too-common recent confessions by young women and lonely wives, *Père* Antoine took the seat in one section of the confessional and slid open the partition when Maggi entered.

---

[11] Father Antoine

Her voice betrayed the sincerity of her guilty feelings and when asked what sin she had committed, Maggi replied simply that she had been with a man. The priest pulled from her that he was a wounded American soldier, that he wasn't married, hadn't proposed marriage to Maggi, and that he would be sent back to America when well enough to travel. Maggi revealed that she hadn't told her mother and didn't want to reveal her shame at home.

Not having thought her situation through, Maggi came across as uncertain about what she was hoping for and so the disappointed but not surprised old priest instructed that she must not see Frank again or have any further contact with him. She sincerely prayed the penance she had been assigned and felt relief in the absolution pronounced by *Père* Antoine.

Five weeks later, in February 1919, Maggi became aware of unusual sensations and began to wonder if she might be pregnant. She was almost certain almost two months after running away from Etretat and Frank and was gripped by ceaseless anxiety about how she would cope. She knew she needed to confide in her mother before she was unable to conceal her condition and began composing a rationale that her mother could accept without adding to her unhappiness. She began to think very often about Frank and believed that *Père* Antoine would understand and agree that it was right that Frank knew of his impending fatherhood but Maggi obeyed her priest's direction.

March 1919 was unusually warm along the Channel coast of France and with the early spring arrived the first local cases of what came to be called the "Spanish Flu." Hundreds of American soldiers waiting in crowded camps to be shipped home and hundreds more still recuperating from war wounds in hospital at Etretat were stricken by what proved to be a disastrously fatal pandemic. Many were dead within 18 hours of first showing flu symptoms; eight to ten died daily. *Madame* Renier caught the flu and quickly became so seriously ill that Maggi put off revealing the news to her mother. Sadly, Maggi nursed her mother till the end in early April, wretched at the injustice of not being able to tell her she would soon be a grandmother.

Now feeling anxious and very much alone, Maggi wanted desperately to be with Frank. She dressed in her nurse's uniform and took the afternoon train from Le Havre to Etretat and waited till dark to walk from the station to the hospital. Her heart pounding in her chest, she entered a side door, trying to appear nonchalant and hoping not to encounter anyone, who would recognize her and her now obvious pregnancy. Carrying a water pitcher and folded towel she took from a table, Maggi walked to Frank's room. A sense of despair washed over her when she discovered a new patient in what had been Frank's bed. At the Nurses' Station down the hall, Maggi picked up the registry and turned pages until she found:

March 17, 1919	Capt. F.S. Rittersberg	Discharged for transportation to US

Dejected and trembling with anxiety, Maggi returned to Le Havre, agonizing over what to do. Locating Frank and surprising him with news of his impending fatherhood seemed impossible obstacles.

After staying alone in her room for three days, Maggi went out to buy some bread and cheese. She discovered that her own former school had just become one of the small clinics that were popping up in the neighborhoods of Le

Havre as the reach of the flu pandemic intensified. With both her mother and Frank now gone, Maggi resolved that something good must come of her own life and she simply showed up at the clinic and just started caring for the sick. Working long hours without days off, Maggi was soon exhausted but carrying on nonetheless. At least her meals were provided at the clinic; a welcome benefit. Weeks passed into months and both doctors and fellow nurses took note of her now-obvious late pregnancy, urging her to get some rest without asking any questions Maggi didn't want to answer.

Her baby boy was born at home in September 1919. Handled by a midwife, the birth was recorded in the church register, Maggi telling the deacon that his name was François Renier and that his father had been in the army. So soon after the ruinous war, no questions were asked and none a few weeks later at the baptism, attended by happy coworkers from the local clinic.

Maggi didn't get to experience much young motherhood. As soon as she felt strong enough, Maggi returned to work at the influenza clinic, leaving little François at a day nursery provided by a nearby convent so that war-widows would be able to work and support their families. Perhaps weakened by her childbirth and punishing work schedule, Maggi became yet another of the flu victims in mid-November and was only permitted a last view of her little son through a window, the doctor forbidding close contact with his sick mother.

Père Antoine ignored his own personal risk, ministering without rest to the dying and bereaved. His attitude was, "God will call me when he deems my work finished and I shall, of course, go obediently." As her end drew near, he heard Maggi's confession and performed the Last Rites. Maggi's final words to *Père* Antoine were, "Find my son's father. His name is Franz Rittersberg, an American captain. He was a patient at Etretat Hospital and has gone home to America. Please find him and tell him he has a son. Please!"

Putting two and two together, the priest recalled Maggi's confession during Christmas Week last year and his admonition that Maggi not see "the man" again. Instinctively believing that the rightful place for Maggi's son was with his father, *Père* Antoine hastened to begin the search for Captain Rittersberg. But where to start?

Without any contact with the Americans and not speaking any English, the old priest considered going himself to Etretat but expected difficulties in suddenly showing up without an introduction and asking delicate questions. He was also reluctant to be away from his terminally ill parishioners. Instead, he wrote a brief letter in French addressed to the *"Chapelaine Americane, Hôpital Militaire, Etretat."* Wrestling with the choice between asking for someone to contact him so that an important message might be passed versus plainly stating Maggi's plea, the priest considered the possibility of his own demise at any time and so simply stated the source of the information, his own witness to Maggi's death, and her urgent wish that Captain Rittersberg be found and notified. *Père* Antoine added that the boy was being cared for at the at *Cloître de Ste Adela*,[12] in Le Havre, where *Mère Supérieure*[13] Bénédicte presided. He signed the letter, "Yours in Christ, *Père* Antoine LeBlanc, FMI."[14]

---

[12] Cloister of Saint Adela

[13] Mother Superior

[14] FMI: Congregation of the Sons of Mary Immaculate

CHAPTER 8

December 1919 - The Search for Frank, Etretat Field Hospital

Chaplain (Major) Louis Bleach thought, at first, that this was yet another unsubstantiated paternity claim against an American soldier but considered it significant that it was a deathbed confession during Extreme Unction and forwarded by a fellow priest. He respected the stationery with the letterhead, *Eglise St. Jean Baptiste*[15] and the signature of *Père* Antoine LeBlanc, FMI. The records clerk in the hospital's administrative office found Frank's file right away and told Father Bleach that he had been discharged from the hospital on March 17th and transported to the Processing Office in Le Havre for immediate embarkation. The clerk had no further information: no ship name, no sailing date, no US port, no reassignment unit for Frank.

Back at Etretat, in his own chapel office, Father Bleach found a roster of chaplains – all of whom he knew – and their scheduled sailing dates back to the US. First Lieutenant Patrick Kenton was next to go. Kenton was scheduled to sail to Philadelphia on January 27th for discharge after which he would assume his pre-war

---

[15] Church of Saint John the Baptist

position at St. Anne's Church in Annapolis. Kenton agreed to take *Père* Antoine's letter and continue the search after his ocean crossing. True to his word, in early February, Kenton started looking for Frank but first asked the wrong questions in the wrong places. No one had any record of a Captain Rittersberg's arrival on a ship anywhere on the US East Coast. He was finally advised to contact the War Department in Washington.

On February 27th, the search for Frank found its way to the desk of Wilbur Morgan, a mid-level supervisor in the office handling reassignments or discharges for Army returnees from France. Morgan located Frank's name in the "Returnees" ledger and notified Kenton that Frank had been assigned to the 305th Tank Brigade at Camp Meade in Maryland.

CHAPTER 9

Camp Meade, Maryland

Frank and his West Point classmate, Dwight Eisenhower had enjoyed a happy reunion. Both now Army majors assigned to the Tank Corps, they had much catching up to do. Ike, whose Stateside assignment was the development of tanks and tank tactics had an endless set of questions about Frank's experiences in France. He obviously envied Frank's combat service in France but tried honestly to learn from his experience. The reunion and tank "shop talk" continued at dinner in the Officers' Mess, joined by their Commanding Officer, Colonel George Patton.

Patton extended a very warm welcome to Frank – loud enough for everyone in the room to hear. He was genuinely pleased that Frank was walking easily and  training to run again. It was very late when they headed to bed. Ike told Frank that he and his wife and son would be moving from nearby

Mark VIII Liberty Tank

Laurel to Post Quarters in a week. "You'll like Mamie," Ike promised.

At work, Patton, Eisenhower, and Frank were completely comfortable with each other. Each a West Point graduate committed to rock-firm principles, each trusted the others' views and judgements and made steady progress during the next six months of 1919 in developing specifications for the first US-built tank – the Mark VIII Liberty.

They were all close and friendly, sharing Christmas and New Year's 1920. The Pattons and Eisenhowers held festive dinners at home and Frank, still living in bachelor's quarters, hosted a dinner at the Officers' Club. At their dinner, George and Bea Patton invited a young lady to fill out the table and for Frank to meet. Frank was polite to her, had no difficulty with conversation, but no romance took seed. At the time, Frank was still subconsciously unready for a relationship, holding himself aloof.

Frank was completely focused on the tank project one morning in March 1920 when a young soldier knocked at his office door to advise that a telephone caller had asked for him at Post Headquarters, leaving a number where he could be reached. "The caller said it was "urgent."

Most Americans in 1920 had little experience with telephones and for Frank, this was his first with an "urgent" call. He walked briskly to the headquarters building and asked a clerk to ring the number that was left for him. It was from Annapolis.

"Franz Rittersberg?" Father Pat Kenton asked and when Frank acknowledged, Kenton volunteered, "Man if you only knew how hard you were to find." Kenton identified himself as a priest at St. Anne's in Annapolis and explained that, as was Frank, he was a recent returnee from the hospital at Etretat, France. He said that he needed to speak with him – face-to-face – right away; it could not be discussed by telephone. With his anxious mind racing in all directions at the mystery, Frank agreed to meet Kenton at the Annapolis station of the WBA Railroad at 1 PM the next day. Frank asked Colonel Patton for the time off and Ike drove him to the station in nearby Odenton.

Kenton spotted Frank's army uniform as soon as he stepped down from the railcar. In the station coffee shop, Kenton cut right to the chase without subjecting Frank to any further suspense. "Franz," he said, word has reached us from Etretat that one of your nurses there has named you as the father of her child."

"Maggi, Marguerite!" Frank interrupted excitedly. He started to ask "When . . ." but Kenton put his hand on Frank's and continued. "I'm afraid the news is not all good. The nurse, Marguerite Renier died in the influenza epidemic soon after her son was born. In her deathbed confession to her priest, she named you as the boy's father and begged that you be notified. The boy is at a convent in Le Havre, where *Mademoiselle* Renier lived."

Speechless for a few seconds, Frank wanted especially to know the boy's birthdate and, hearing that is was in September 1919, did quick math and realized it must have been their tryst near the shore. In Frank's situation, most wartime returnees from overseas would feel an immediate knee-jerk "not mine" conclusion but lights came on for Frank and he knew inside that it was true.

39

Father Kenton gave Frank all the letters and papers he had accumulated during his search, wished him good luck and offered his further services, if Frank needed.

Back on the train for the short run to Odenton, Frank's

head was a jumble of what to do, how to do it, whom to tell, and what to say. Once on post, his military discipline automatically kicked in and he realized he needed to inform Colonel Patton; as they shared a solemn oath never "To lie, cheat, or steal or tolerate anyone who did."[16]

Colonel George Patton

"Well, I'll be damned," Patton said. "Sure, I remember that pretty French nurse and I remember telling you I thought she liked you." Pinching his chin, Patton looked squarely at Frank. "Is the boy yours?"

"I believe so. It was just after Christmas. The war was over, it was a happy time. We really liked each other and I felt very close to her, thought seriously about bringing her back with me. Didn't realize it then but I guess I loved her. We drank some champagne and things just went further than I ever planned. I really don't remember how it happened. I'm pretty certain it was her first time; it was for me. But she ran off right afterwards and I couldn't find her although I never stopped looking while I was still in France. On the ship coming home, I reckoned that she didn't want to see me again so I decided to put it all

---

[16] The West Point Honor Code

behind me and concentrate on the future." Frank put his head down with his face in both hands. "I feel so guilty, so ashamed. She had to go through having a baby alone and now she's dead."

"What are you going to do about the boy?" Patton challenged.

"I don't know. I haven't begun to think"

"If he's your son, you have to fetch him back here. Can't leave him over there with France in ruins and no father. It's the right thing to do." Patton was Frank's commanding officer. They shared a sacred oath. Patton's expression was stern, reminding Frank about "honor" without pronouncing the word.

Next morning in the office, Frank laid his soul bare before Ike, whose face revealed that he was already in problem-solving mode. Ike was in lock-step agreement with Patton that "fetching the boy back was the right thing to do" but Ike was already thinking through the difficulties of making a trip back across the Atlantic – and with an infant!

Major Dwight D. Eisenhower

"Would the boy need a passport? Could he get a French passport or would a US passport be possible? Getting to France would be easy but ships sailing West were fully booked with Doughboys coming home. If Frank went, what did he know about taking care of a baby – and at sea?" Should Frank take a Nanny with him? Would having a Nanny along complicate getting Westbound passage?"

Back in their quarters, Ike filled Mamie in, using an upbeat tone, "Icky will have a new friend." At first, Mamie was briefly scandalized but, as a mother herself, grasped the priorities and bypassed unhelpful judgmental conclusions.

She wasted no time in discussing the situation with Bea Patton, the colonel's wife. Both were very fond of Frank and accepted that "these things happen in wartime." It had already been granted that Frank loved Marguerite and wanted to bring her back so, "Where do we go from here?

Both ladies were excited at the prospect of helping with a baby and quickly added to their discussion all the baby-things Frank was going to need and what they needed to teach him.

1920s: Bea Patton and Mamie Eisenhower (Wikimedia Commons)

Major and Mrs Eisenhower with "Icky"

CHAPTER 10

April 1920 – Understanding Franz Rittersberg, Sr. – Stu's Grandfather [We'll get back to Frank and Stu soon!]

Franz Sr. was a West Point graduate, Class of 1892. He was recruited to play football on the academy's first-ever team, organized and coached by a fellow-member of Franz Sr.'s company, Cadet Dennis Michie.[17] After graduation and six years of Army duty at various posts, Franz Sr. and Michie both served in Cuba during the Spanish-American War. Franz Sr. distinguished himself at the Battle of *El Caney* but came home suffering from a serious case of Yellow Fever that affected his liver, causing life-long flare-ups. Following that war and Franz Sr's return to the US, he served in a succession of infantry units, winning promotions to positions of increased responsibility and a reputation for capability and leadership. Franz' close friend Dennis, however, was killed in action in Cuba.

---

[17] The football gridiron at West Point named "Michie Field" (now "Michie Stadium") is dedicated to the memory of Dennis Michie (1870–1898), who was instrumental in starting the Army football program while a cadet at the Academy. A member of the Class of 1892, Michie organized, managed, and coached the first football team at West Point in 1890.

In 1916, Franz Sr. was stationed at Fort Bliss, Texas on the staff of General John J. Pershing and met Lieutenant George Patton, who rode with Pershing into Mexico in pursuit of Pancho Villa. He had then retired from the Army and returned to the Harrisburg farm shortly before his son was shipped to France. Franz Sr. was invited by friends to join the local Loyal Order of Moose lodge. At a lodge dinner, he met Senator James Davis, who encouraged Franz Sr. to be active in Moose philanthropic projects. Franz Sr. became a generous contributor for the rest of his days.

After having seen Frank in Pennsylvania, right after his son's return from the war, Franz Sr. was highly displeased to get his letter of explanation in February at home in Harrisburg. He was very much more disappointed in his son than he was happy to have become a grandfather. As would be expected, Franz Sr. was immediately full of tough questions that he put into a return letter to his son. Among them were Frank's certainty that the boy was his and what did he plan to do.

Frank sent his father a Western Union Telegram:

> YES HE'S MINE STOP I WANT TO GO GET HIM STOP

Frank's father answered immediately by telegram:

> MEET ME BALTIMORE PENN STATION SUNDAY
> FIVE PM STOP

Frank knew he didn't need to reply to his father's instruction. For his part, Franz Sr. knew Frank would meet his train. When Frank told Colonel Patton that his father was coming, Patton insisted on driving Frank to Baltimore to bring him back to Camp Meade. "I remember your father from the Pancho Villa Expedition back in 1916. Bet he'll remember me!"

On Sunday, George Patton drove Frank to Baltimore and met his father. Patton and Frank Sr had a mini-reunion but Patton respectfully called Frank's father, "Sir," deferring to the older man's date of rank as a colonel. Franz Sr. complemented Patton's Buick sedan during the drive down US Route 1 toward Camp Meade and reviewed their shared early history, obviously waiting to speak privately with his son.

Franz Sr's hoped-for privacy would have to wait. Once inside Camp Meade, Patton drove directly to his Post quarters on 4th Street, where his wife, Bea, had prepared a welcoming dinner. Mamie and Ike were already there and Patton Introduced Franz Sr. as an old buddy. Franz Sr. also remembered meeting Ike when he attended the Army-Rutgers game in 1912. A broadly smiling Eisenhower shook Franz Sr's hand firmly, also naturally addressing him as "sir." Patton offered Franz Sr. a glass of his home-brewed beer and led him to show off his brewing set-up.

As soon as Patton was alone with Frank's father, he suggested: "I sense that you're disappointed in Frank but I wouldn't be too hard on the boy. I was in the hospital with Frank – in the next bed actually – and the girl was my nurse too. Pretty girl, very proper and not at all flirty. Awfully hard-working with little time off; they couldn't have had much time alone. I'm certain she was in love with Frank and I think he felt the same. My guess is that, with his release from the hospital coming up, they found a private moment and things just went out of control. Frank has completely opened up to me and I know he's deeply troubled but I give him credit for wanting to do the honorable thing. He was a very brave and competent officer in France and I'm damned-well proud of him. I'm going to help him all I can and hope you will too."

The dinner went flowingly, punctuated by lively conversation. The men drank lots of Patton's beer and, when Bea and Mamie cleared the table and disappeared into the kitchen, Ike ran next door to his own quarters to fetch a bottle of his home-brewed gin. The four relaxed West Pointers discussed Army football in Franz Sr's day versus Frank's and Ike's era, tanks, the League of Nations, until Frank asked, "Pop, are you getting sleepy?" In truth, the beer and gin had brought him to a relaxed, drowsy state. Patton drove both Rittersbergs to the BOQ[18], where a VIP room had been reserved for the visitor.

After Patton dropped them off, Franz Sr. put his hands on Frank's shoulders, as he did when he saw him off to France. "Son, it's real late. Let's talk in the morning."

At breakfast next morning, in the Officers' Mess, Franz Sr. was still feeling last night's alcohol. "Never had home-made gin before. I thought it was pretty good," he allowed. Father and son spent almost two hours discussing the main subject at hand. Frank repeated for his father what he had confided in Patton, emphasizing Maggi's character, her nursing care of him, and his sense of a shared love.

---

[18] Bachelor Officers Quarters

"I keep telling myself that I should have had better self-control and that I deserve all the blame but a child – my son, your grandson - came from it. Even if France wasn't a mess, I just know he belongs here – with us.

Won over by Frank's sincerity and the moral support he was getting from his Army "family", Franz Sr. acquiesced, "If this boy is our blood, I'm in full agreement with you. If we go forward with bringing him home, there must never be any second-guessing, just a done-deal. I can sign up for that; can you?"

"Of course," Frank acknowledged, hugging his father, both tearing-up quietly.

"I wish your mother was still with us," Franz Sr. mused. "I'm sure she would have been a great help in what lies before us. And she'd have loved a little grandson. I'll have to do her part for our grandson."

The discussion next turned to logistics of bringing the baby to America. And finances.

The Early Years of Franz Rittersberg Sr. – Stu's Grandfather

In 1891, while an upperclassman at West Point, Franz's own father died, bequeathing his two, already-married, older sisters generous sums he had put aside for them plus various heirlooms he knew they would treasure. He left the farm near Harrisburg to Franz. With solid commitment to entering the Army and not at all knowledgeable of or interested in farming, Franz was overwhelmed by the prospect of suddenly running such a huge enterprise from afar. Even keeping on Mr. Turner, his father's long-time manager, Franz was staggered by the prospect of having so many seasonal employees, so many horses and mules, so much attention to be paid to payrolls, taxes, timely planting and selling, and constant worries about insects and the weather. He chose a military career instead of farming.

His father's lawyer arranged the sale of most of the farm's acreage, keeping the main old stone house and just two acres of land. Suddenly wealthy, Franz deposited two-thirds of the sale proceeds in the First Pennsylvania Bank, where his family had been depositors for decades. With the remaining one-third, he bought shares in the Pennsylvania Railroad. Confident that the money was safe, he returned to West Point and graduated in the Class of 1892.

In a traditional "arch of sabres" wedding at the West Point Chapel on Graduation Day, Franz married Anna Katherine Hartmann, who had just graduated from Franklin & Marshall. Their son, Franz Steuben Rittersberg, Jr. was born in 1893. First Lieutenant Rittersberg went to Cuba in 1898 and returned as a Captain. While in Cuba, he contracted Yellow Fever. It would trouble him for the rest of his life.

Franz held various staff assignments involving logistics and, except for occasional liver issues lingering from his earlier bout with Yellow Fever, life was trouble-free until he returned home one evening to find his wife, Anna, dead in the bathtub. A faulty water heater in a closet of their small bathroom had leaked Carbon Monoxide gas, which killed her. Franz could never reconcile her untimely death; she appeared so peaceful in the tub as if she had simply fallen asleep. Always very close to his mother, Franz Jr. (called "Frank") was hit hard by her sudden death. He would realize in later life that his mother had been the only woman or girl with whom he was ever close and, coupled with his attendance at all-male schools, was never involved in serious romantic relationships, concentrating instead on studies and sports.

Franz raised Frank alone and enrolled him in schools near Harrisburg. In 1907, Frank. entered Carson Long Military Academy in nearby Bloomfield, PA. An all-around athlete, Frank played baseball and football and ran track. He was well-prepared to enter West Point in 1911, where he played football with cadets he would later soldier with: Dwight Eisenhower, Omar Bradley, and Norman Cota.

1913 USMA Football Team. Ike is 2nd from left; Bradley is 2nd from right.

The war in Europe that had started in the summer of 1914 was very much on the minds of the whole Corps of Cadets at the academy. Frank, Omar Bradley and Ike discussed endlessly among themselves and others in their company the possibility that the US would enter the war and get them into the fight. As the Class of 1915 was getting ready for their graduation ceremony and commissioning as Second Lieutenants, news arrived in May that the RMS Lusitania had been sunk by a German torpedo, killing almost 1200 passengers, Americans among them. The cadets were outraged and ready, as a man, to head for France. They would, however, have to wait till June 1917 – fully two years.

After graduation, both Frank and Ike were assigned to Camp Meade in Maryland with the task of developing the Army's new Tank Corps. Both read everything they could find about the war and confidently expected orders for France but only Frank went "Over There" while a disappointed Ike was posted to another Stateside assignment.

[Now back to Frank, who is ready to leave for France]

CHAPTER 11

March 1920 - The Fetch Trip

Frank went up to Baltimore, where he took a B&O train to Philadelphia. A taxi brought him to the Snyder Avenue pier, where he boarded the SS Radnor, a wartime troopship now reverted to civilian service. Frank travelled "light" for himself but brought along a small steamer trunk full of "baby things" packed by Bea Patton and Mamie Eisenhower. Much of the collection were hand-me-downs from both ladies' now-older children, Ruth Ellen Patton and "Icky" Eisenhower. Frank's head spun from the stream of "do and don't" instructions that poured not just from the experienced mothers but also from Patton and Ike.

Tugboats pushed the aging SS Radnor, much in need of scraping and painting, into the main channel of the Delaware River and she slowly made her way to where the river widened to become Delaware Bay and then out into the Atlantic. Frank stood at the stern rail until the Cape Henlopen lighthouse slipped beneath the horizon. He certainly hadn't planned on returning to France so soon.

SS Radnor

The next morning, a room steward brought Frank a Radiogram in a yellow envelope. It was from his father advising Frank that, when he arrived in Le Havre, he would be contacted by Eric Wood. Wood, an American with experience as an embassy attaché in Paris, had served in the British Army in France until the US joined the war in 1917. He then had been a Lieutenant Colonel in Paris and helped there to organize the new American Legion. Wood had many friends, who could prove helpful to Frank.

One of Frank's father's contacts had recommended Wood as a capable guide for arranging Frank's departure from France with the baby. Wood was approached by the father's contact in a CCC Cablegram, which briefly outlined Frank's mission and identified Frank as a wounded Silver Star holder. Already feeling lonesome out at sea with likely complications ahead, Frank was relieved and looked forward to meeting Wood.

Frank sent a Radiogram of his own – in French - to *Père* Antoine at the Le Havre church named in the letterhead of the priest's letter to Etretat Hospital after Maggi's death. Frank advised that he had been informed of the boy's birth and of Maggi's death and was coming in a fortnight to get his son. The Atlantic can be cold, stormy and quite rough in March. The SS Radnor was slow – only able to make 10 knots in good conditions. Frank estimated that they would make Le Havre in eleven more days.

On March 23rd, Eric Wood met the ship and gave Frank a very friendly greeting free of any implied judgement concerning an illegitimate birth. Wood explained that he had been in the same infantry unit as a comrade, who knew Frank's father. "Glad to help any way I can. What do you want to do first?"

Frank pulled out Père Antoine's original letter. "I'd like to go right away to St. John Baptiste Church at 139 *Rue Theophile Gautier*" to see the priest, who knows where my son is."

"OK," agreed Wood. "I think we can find it." "Let's take my car. It's right outside and I have a city map. By the way, I reserved a room for you at the *Hôtel la Manche*. We can check you in there later."

They found the ancient church after a couple of wrong turns. *Père* Antoine was out, expected back in an hour. Frank and Wood crossed the street to the *L'Ombre de l'Eglise* sidewalk café and ordered coffee, keeping a watch for Father Antoine's return. During the wait, Woods told Frank that his was not the first case of expediting a French national's emigration to the US. "Usually, it's a Doughboy wanting to take his new French bride home.

I also know of one other American planning to take a child but I believe that was an adoption. Do you have any documentation proving that the you are the child's father?"

"The only thing I have is the priest's letter explaining that the boy's mother said he was my son in her deathbed confession. The priest signed the letter - - see here?" Frank held out the letter for Wood to see. "Will that carry any weight?"

Church of St. John Baptiste, Le Havre

Wood turned both his palms upward. "We'll see. I will interview the priest myself and, if he will sign the passport application form I have with me, the American Consulate here in Le Havre can have a passport for the boy the next day."

"Gee, that sounds swell!" Frank said with relief and took a sip of the strong black coffee as Wood asked, "Is that our priest now?"

Père Antoine was getting off his bicycle. Walking slowly and with difficulty, he headed for a side door. Frank and Wood caught up with him just as he was about to enter.

"Bonjour mon Père. Je m'appelle Commandant Frank Rittersberg. Et c'est mon ami, Eric Wood.[19] Did you receive my telegram?"

---

[19] Hello, Father. I am Major Frank Rittersberg and this my friend, Eric Wood.

The priest was expecting Frank and politely asked to speak with him privately. He had many questions.

"Are you Catholic?" Frank was asked. "Do you acknowledge that you sinned with Marguerite?" "Would you like me to hear your confession before we discuss your son? "If you are permitted to take the boy to America, will you raise him in the Church?"

Frank made his confession, feeling very humbled but nonetheless grateful that *Père* Antoine was helping him. When those formalities were complete, Frank asked when he could see his son and was answered, "Tomorrow morning." Then to Wood, come with your car at 9:00 o'clock and we will go to the Cloister of Sainte Adela. I will introduce you to the *Mère Supérieure*."

Next Frank asked where Maggi was buried and could *Père* Antoine tell him where to find her grave.

With a pained expression, the priest replied that she was laid to rest in the churchyard, just outside. "Come, I will show you."

The three of them went out among the gravestones as *Père* Antoine explained, "Marguerite was a very good, very special person. After she fled the hospital at Etretat, she came home – here – during the worst of the Spanish Flu. She cared for so many, even when with child. The flu took her as well but she died with a clear conscience. I gave her unction myself. The boy - her son and your son - must be a living memorial to a good daughter of the Church, a good daughter of France. Do you accept your responsibility?"

They reached a corner of the churchyard with obviously recently-dug graves but there were no headstones or even temporary markers.

"Alas, there were so many," the old priest lamented. I'm afraid there was no time and no one to manage so many burials." Gesturing with a sweep of his arm, *Père* Antoine indicated, "She is here somewhere. Among her neighbors. One day, perhaps we will be able to put up a proper memorial with all the names." *Père* Antoine took a card from the bible he was holding and handed it to Frank. "When I learned that you were coming, I copied some information from the Church records that you may need someday."

> *Nom d'enfant* – Marguerite Paulette Renier
>
> *Date de naissance* – 8 Août 1899
>
> *Date de mort* – 16 Novembre 1919
>
> *Nom de Père* – François Maxime Renier
>
> *Nom de Mère* – Paulette Claire (Dubois) Renier
>
> *Adresse du domicile* - 88 Rue de Molière, Havre

Frank read the card, completely choked, unable to make a sound. He stood with head bowed, feeling deep sorrow. Father Antoine put his arm around Frank's shoulder. "Make certain that your son will know and respect his mother's memory." Having maintained his composure until that point, Maggi's smile appeared in his memory. Frank sensed that he had foolishly lost something he really needed, leaving an unfilled hole in his soul. Bitter tears rolled down his cheeks.

Next morning, Wood first picked up Frank and then Father Antoine, who gave directions to the Cloister of Ste. Adela. Mother Superior Bénédicte was waiting for them in the chapel. Her demeanor was cool and formal. *Père* Antoine introduced Frank and Eric Wood and then whispered something privately, after which the Mother Superior nodded and replied, *"Oui, d'accord* [20]*"* and moved to a side door, which she opened. Sisters Ursula and Annunciata followed her to where the three men stood.

Sister Ursula was carrying a blanket-wrapped, sleeping child and when motioned to do so by her Mother Superior, held out the boy to Frank.

Frank had never before held a child in his arms and felt clumsy. Afraid to move one hand to turn his son to see his face, he stood immobile. Sister Annunciata reached over and helped turn the child, giving Frank his first look and the boy awoke and looked at his father.

A warmly-smiling Sister Ursula said to her Mother Superior, "He is certainly the father. Look: they have the same eyes!" *"Oui, sans doute,"* [21] she agreed.

"Let us pray," intoned *Père* Antoine.

After *Père* Antoine's "Amen," Frank turned and put the boy in a surprised Wood's arms. He reached into his pocket and pulled out two fifty dollar gold pieces. He gave one to Mother Superior Bénédicte and the other to

---

[20] Yes, agreed

[21] Yes, without doubt

Père Antoine, telling each individually, "*Merci tant!*[22] To help with your work."

Frank and Wood went out to Wood's car. "I picked up a pram from my neighbor for you. It's a *Magnat-Debon* – top of the line. You owe me four francs," Wood joked. "It's in the trunk." Driving away from the church, Wood said soberly, "You're a brave man. You're gonna' have your hands full and you'll be on your own. I must get back to Paris but will stop by our consulate here this afternoon. I'll have Monsieur Delacroix issue your son's passport and get it over to your hotel this evening. By the way, what is the boy's full name?"

Frank had decided on the answer to Wood's question on the voyage coming over and replied firmly, "Franz Steuben Rittersberg the Third. But I'm going to call him Fuzzy."

"OK; Just what I would have guessed." "I'll fill it in the passport application that Father Antoine signed. Now, let's get you and Franz the Third over to your hotel. By the way, tell the Concierge you will need some warm milk. Do you have baby bottles and diapers in that steamer trunk you brought off the ship?"

"Yes, friends back in Maryland put together about everything I should need till I get back."

"You should be all set then, I have you booked on White Star's RMS Olympic, sailing from Cherbourg tomorrow

---

[22] Thank you so much

at 6pm. Tell the Concierge you need a taxi to the train station and a First Class ticket on the 9 o'clock express to Cherbourg. That will get you there at 3:30. Then take a cab to the pier. You should be able to go right on board. At the gangway, tell them you and your son are on the passenger list. Your father made all the arrangements through their New York office."

At the *Hôtel La Manche*, Frank started getting to know his son. He slept very little that night between feedings, diaper-changes, amid the swirl of "do's and don'ts" he was told by Mamie and Bea. Getting to the ship in Cherbourg was easy except for fitting the pram into the taxi, which wound up being tied on the *Citroen's* rear.

The Olympic sailed from Cherbourg on March 27th, heading west. On board, the White Star staff was very attentive, providing whatever Frank needed. He was getting the hang of

RMS Olympic

caring for a five-month old boy, who was already able to turn himself over and recognized his father with smiles and cooing. Father and son did twice daily pram rides around the Promenade Deck, earning approving nods and smiles from many of their female shipmates. Frank was surprised by how many ladies seemed to enjoy holding his son. He thought often of Maggi.

In the First Class dining room, Frank, wearing his Army Major's uniform with his war ribbons, ate with Fuzzy on his lap. They were seated at a table for eight people, including Miss Elizabeth Carrington from Boston. Frank saw Elizabeth as a most attractive young woman, accompanying an elderly aunt home after they had attended a wedding in England. Noting Frank's clumsy attempts at feeding himself while holding the baby, she offered to hold him and seemed to enjoy speaking baby-talk and dandling him. When Elizabeth reached to take Fuzzy, Frank caught a whiff of her perfume, which reminded him of the *Brises de Violettes* he had given Maggi. It steered his thoughts to a love he had lost – so foolishly.

At their table was older veteran of the Spanish-American War, Colonel Thomas Spooner. The colonel spoke aloud to Frank so that all could hear, "I see you were in France and have a Silver Star and a Purple Heart. Tell us about those." Very modestly, Frank described being wounded in a tank battle at St. Mihiel and recovering at the Etretat Field Hospital.

Frank also told his table-mates that the boy was his son, that his mother had died, and that they were going home to America. When asked the boy's name, Frank explained the "senior-junior-the third" sequence, adding, "I'm calling him 'Fuzzy" because 'the third' seems so pretentious for a little boy."

Over the next few days, Elizabeth spent a lot of time being helpful and friendly to Frank, who was oblivious to all her subtle signals of an invitation to a shipboard romance. He thought she was very nice and appreciated the assistance but starting a relationship was not on his mind, especially with Maggi's baby there.

CHAPTER 12

April 1920 - New York

The Olympic docked in New York and Fuzzy's grandfather met him and his father on the dock. "He sure looks like you Frank!"

A young immigration officer at the pier seemed puzzled that Frank, in his uniform, and the boy were travelling on separate passports. Instead of trying to explain, Frank said that he had additional documents in his luggage and held Fuzzy out to the officer. "Here, hold him for moment. Sorry he's a little stinky; I haven't had a chance to change him since we cleared our stateroom this morning."

"That's OK," the young man said, rubber-stamping both passports. "Welcome back soldier. Next in line!"

They took a taxi to the Wolcott Hotel, near Penn Station, where Grandpa Franz had booked a suite. They enjoyed a happy 2-day family get-together, which included Grandpa relearning diaper-changing techniques and feeding a little boy. Frank's leave was up and he needed to get back to Camp Meade.

Grandpa Franz saw them off at Penn Station. Ike met their train at Penn Station in Baltimore, smiling happily, loading everything into his 1919 Ford for the drive down to Camp Meade.

A surprise was waiting for Frank: during his absence, Patton and Ike had quarters assigned for Frank and Fuzzy right across from theirs on 4th Street and had moved all Frank's stuff over from his BOQ room. They even bought a crib and set up Fuzzy's new room.

For the first few days, Fuzzy was kept by either Bea Patton or Mamie Eisenhower until Frank found a woman in Odenton, who would take care of Fuzzy and do some housekeeping.

CHAPTER 13

May 1920, Camp Meade, Maryland

Frank was settled-in with his 8 month-old son and enjoyed buying furniture, clothes and baby toys. That spring was an idyllic time: The Pattons, Eisenhowers and Rittersbergs were close-knit – a veritable family. The Pattons' two girls, the Eisenhowers' son Icky and Fuzzy were together for hours almost every day. On Colonel Patton's advice, Frank bought a new Buick Touring Car – spacious enough for Fuzzy's pram. One summer evening, drinking George Patton's home brew, Ike reminisced. "Funny how much we've experienced in common. I hurt my left knee tackling Jim Thorpe. George, you were shot in the left leg. And Frank, your left leg was messed up at St. Mihiel. They all nodded and drank to good fortune.

Toward the end of the summer, Frank took two weeks leave and drove up into Pennsylvania to visit Grandpa Rittersberg in Harrisburg. It was a happy reunion and Grandpa obviously enjoyed his grandson but regretted aloud several times that Fuzzy's Grandma couldn't be with them. Frank took note of his father's obvious discomfort from recurrent liver problems caused by the Yellow Fever he caught back in 1898.

Back at Camp Meade, Frank contemplated his good life. He loved the Army, was dedicated to his job, and fit right in with his neighbors and co-workers. But the Army broke up the happy tribe later that year, transferring Colonel Patton to Fort Meyer in Northern Virginia. It wasn't that far away but the close-knit family-like neighbors accepted the separation in sadness. Frank and Ike continued to work well together and Fuzzy and Icky remained constant playmates.

If anything, Frank and Ike drew closer. They were consciously non-political but, in their discussions, favored Warren Harding's positions and were satisfied by the result of the 1920 election. They celebrated Thanksgiving at the Eisenhowers' on November 25th and listened to the first college football game broadcast on nationwide radio by WTAW, between Texas U and Mechanical College of Texas. They enjoyed a happy Christmas in the Officers Club and exchanged gifts later at home.

Detail of a group photo of the 17th Tank Battalion at Camp Meade in 1920. Colonel George Patton and Major Dwight Eisenhower are in the 2nd row, third and fourth from the left, respectively. If he had been real, Frank Rittersberg would have been in the photo.

Unimaginable tragedy struck days later at New Years 1921: Icky came down with Scarlet Fever and died in the Camp Meade Hospital on January 2nd. Ike and Mamie were crushed. Frank mourned with them. Fuzzy was too young to understand but obviously missed his usual playmate. Frank was tormented by the injustice of it: little Icky suddenly taken from Mamie and Ike for no reason, causing them such anguish. Fuzzy, suddenly robbed of his familiar playmate. Himself awash in such pangs of helplessness. Frank remembered Ike's support when the news of his having a son in France was first received. And Mamie and Ike stepping up like an aunt and uncle when they were needed. Frank felt he wanted

67

to do something, anything to ease his friends' pain. He felt powerless. Guilty.

Life changed in the next several months and the outlook for 1921 offered little of the earlier contentment enjoyed in the 4th Street neighborhood. Later in 1921, Ike was alerted for transfer to Panama and he and Mamie bid their farewells to Frank and Fuzzy. Frank stayed on in his old job at Camp Meade, really missing his buddies and starting to feel burned out. His own transfer alert came a few months after the Eisenhowers left. He was going halfway around the world to the Philippines. Immediately, Frank had mixed emotions about the overseas assignment. He decided to drive up to Harrisburg for discussions with his father.

Grandpa Franz wasn't doing well when Frank and Fuzzy arrived. His liver was acting up, affecting his appetite, his digestion and his sleep. Frank thought his father looked yellowish and had aged a couple of years since he last saw him. Grandpa Franz was clearly unhappy about Frank's impending transfer so far away and tried not to sound selfish. When Frank confessed that he wasn't anxious to go to the Philippines, discussion of the Pennsylvania National Guard eventually came up. After four hours of non-stop discussion, Frank reached a decision: he would resign his commission in the Regular US Army and his father would ask his friend, Governor Bill Sproul to appoint him to the Pennsylvania National Guard.

Grandpa Franz seemed pleased with Frank's decision but asked him several times in the next two days if he were sure. For Frank, it was good that he was asked. It made him review his rationale, which became stronger each time around. A bonus point in Frank's mind was that

Grandpa Franz wouldn't miss an important phase of his only grandson's growing up.

One again, Grandpa repeated, "I do wish your mother was still with us. She'd be so happy to know you and Fuzzy were going to be nearby."

His father's words made the image of his mother at the kitchen stove come immediately to Frank's mind. It was the most vivid memory of her face that he retained. His thoughts then switched to Maggi's face and smile and Frank regretted again that he didn't even have a picture of her. He confessed to his father: "Maggi should be here too. I'll never forgive myself for being so dumb, so out of control. I keep telling myself what I should have done after kissing her was just to ask her to come home with me. That's all. I'll never understand it. I'm sure she would have said 'yes.' We'd have gotten married and had Fuzzy a little later. She never had a chance to really know him. Maggi would have loved it here, so peaceful and green. She was such a good girl; I'm sure you would've liked her."

CHAPTER 14

1922 Frank joins the Pennsylvania National Guard

Frank wrote letters of explanation to George Patton and Dwight Eisenhower, hinting that he would value their counsel. Both supported his decision and wished him success. Frank's Regular Army resignation and Pennsylvania National Guard commissioning were both to be effective on January 1, 1922. He and Fuzzy moved out of their Camp Meade quarters and drove to Harrisburg in time to spend Christmas with Grandpa Franz in the big old farmhouse. Bertha, a live-in housekeeper/cook had been with Grandpa Franz for several years and she helped in choosing a live-in Nanny for Fuzzy.

Frank took up his new job as Deputy Chief of Operations and Training with an office in the State Capitol Building on 3rd Street, just four miles from home. As an additional duty, he was appointed Chief of Operations, 28th Infantry Division, which had been federalized in 1917 and fought in France. In 1919, the 28th ID was demobilized and reposted to Harrisburg. Frank fit in easily with the men of the 28th; his Silver Star and service ribbons identified him as "one of theirs." Grandpa Franz also had friends in the Division, whose battle history included service in Cuba during the Spanish-American War.

The passing years were agreeably uneventful in the Rittersberg household. Fuzzy attended an elementary school close to home. He enjoyed books and playing with toy soldiers. In nice weather, could be found lying on the back lawn, watching clouds, circling hawks, and the occasional biplane buzzing across the sky while wondering what it was like up there. During his summer and holiday breaks, Grandpa Franz spent a lot of time with and became very close to his grandson. They went fishing and swam from a bank of the Susquehanna River and enjoyed radio dramas in the living room. In 1927, Grandpa showed Fuzzy on a map the route Lindbergh followed across the Atlantic. Fuzzy was full of questions.

They went downtown to the Pennsylvania State Library and Fuzzy got his own library card. In frequent trips, Fuzzy checked-out *Above the Bright Blue Sky* by Elliott Springs and *The Greatest Man in the World* by James Thurber – both aviation stories. Fuzzy had a keen interest in flying adventures and, when they were playing at the Rialto Theater, Grandpa took him to see *Dawn Patrol, Central Airport, Hell's Angels, The Eagle and the Hawk, and Parachute Jumper.* Fuzzy became adept at folding paper airplanes that flew straighter and further than his friends'.

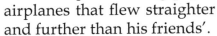

As a 10th birthday present, Grandpa, Frank and Fuzzy went to the Pennsylvania State Fair to see the airshow, complete with aerobatics,

wing-walkers, and parachute jumpers. As a special treat, Fuzzy got his first airplane ride in an old Curtiss Jenny. Being up among big puffy clouds and looking down at the river, the city, and his home were thrilling. Fuzzy was forever hooked. Soon stick-built airplane models were hanging from his bedroom ceiling and he learned to draw various recognizable aircraft types. When asked what he wanted to be when he grew up, his ready answer was always the same: "a pilot." The boy could never resist looking up when he heard an airplane engine.

Grandpa Franz gave Fuzzy a telescope on a tripod for Christmas. It took Fuzzy's breath away when he first saw craters on the moon and Jupiter with four of its moons. It was the start of a life-long interest in astronomy.

In 1930, following his father's footsteps, Fuzzy entered Carson Long Military Academy, the oldest preparatory boarding school and military academy in the United States. The day before moving to the dorm at Carson Long at nearby New Bloomfield, Fuzzy stood up straight in front of his father and grandfather.

"I don't want to be called 'Fuzzy' any more. The kids at school are always teasing me about it. And some of the kids, who know my full name, make fun of me being the 'third' by calling me 'the turd.'"

"What should we call you then," Frank asked.

"Well I can't be 'Franz' or 'Junior;' those are already taken. I want to use my middle name and have people call me 'Stu.'"

Father and grandfather chuckled in agreement From that day on, the boy was called "Stu." But it wasn't to be so simple. The very first day at Carson Long, freshman cadets stood an inspection in their new uniforms, standing in front of their bunks. Inspecting was Third-year Cadet Raymond Stokes, six inches taller than Stu and outweighing him by twenty-five pounds. Resplendent in his academy dress uniform with stripes, Stokes moved from bunk to bunk, asking each cadet's name. He expected cadets, standing at rigid attention, to answer loudly and to pronounce "Sir" with emphasis.

When Stu answered, Stokes tilted his head back and laughed loudly enough for all to hear. "What, like Stupid? I think we'll call you Stupid! OK Stupid?"

Stu's sudden right cross caught Stoke's chin solidly and the bigger boy was caught completely off-guard and off-balance. He stumbled backward and fell in an undignified sprawl. Stu's dorm mates erupted in whoops and applause. Stokes regained his feet and quick-stepped out of the dorm.

His bunk-mates gathered around Stu, waving fists, clapping him on the back. Somebody said it first and then everybody was chanting it. "Beefstew, Beefstew, Beefstew."

Retired Warrant Officer Benson, Commandant of Cadets, gave Stu twenty-five demerits for striking a cadet NCO and had him walk two hour punishment tours for five days. Stokes received five demerits for "unbecoming conduct" and Benson took a stripe from him. No one at the academy ever poked fun at Stu's name again and "Beefstew" stuck.

During summer vacation in 1931, Grandpa Franz took Stu to see his first Major League Baseball game. They had seen some Harrisburg Senators (Class B) games at Island Field but Stu looked forward to seeing the Philadelphia Phillies, his favorite team at home, which he followed on the radio. On July 11, they went by train to Philadelphia and then in a cab to the old Baker Bowl. There was a doubleheader that day but Grandpa said they could only see the first game because they needed to make a 6 o'clock train back to Harrisburg. It was a dismal disappointment for Stu: the New York Giants crushed the Phillies 23 to 5. Thereafter, Stu switched from the Phillies and became a long-time Philadelphia Athletics fan.

1933

Grandpa Franz gave Stu two books as a present for his 14th birthday that profoundly influenced the trajectory of his later life. *Southern Mail* and *Night Flight* by French aviator Antoine de Saint-Exupéry firmly seized the boy's attention. The two flying adventures became his favorites and he reread both many times. Later, he would read and reread Saint-Exupéry's *Flight to Arras* and *Wind, Sand and Stars*. One winter evening in 1935, in front of the fire, Grandpa Franz, Frank and 16 year-old Stu were in casual conversation, which led to the boy's favorite reading.

"Maybe it's your French blood that makes you like Saint-Exupéry," Grandpa suggested. Stu didn't reply or ask any questions but he began wondering inside. Some days later, when alone with Frank, Stu came out with the question. "Pop, I know my mother was French. What happened to her?"

Frank told his son the whole story, saving the "unmarried" point for a follow-up question, if it ever came. He emphasized Maggi's caring goodness and selfless work ethic. Remembering *Père* Antoine's charge, Frank said that she was a good daughter of France. He confessed to thinking often of "his nurse" and of seeing reminders of her in Stu's face and smile.

"Someday, we will take a trip to France and go to Le Havre, where your mother lived. Learn French well in school to be ready for that trip. And remember what Thomas Jefferson said. *Chaque homme a deux patries: la sienne et la France.*[23] That applies doubly to you."

Back in school, Stu progressed well at Carson Long. His best subjects academically were English composition, history, French and science. He passed all his math classes but struggled with algebra and trigonometry. He played baseball and football and was on the academy's rifle team. Stu excelled in Military Science, graduating with honors in 1936. His good grades and family connections gained Stu an appointment to West Point by Grandpa's old friend, US Senator James J. Davis.[24] Grandpa Franz and Jim Davis had been friends since Davis met him in the Etretat hospital as chairman of the Loyal Order of Moose War Relief Commission in 1918.

1936

The cadets in Stu's class were acutely aware of the geopolitical situation in Manchuria, Africa, and Europe where Japan's Fumimoro Kanoe, Mussolini, and Hitler were growing powerful armies and seizing neighboring

---

[23] "Every man has two countries, his own and France."

[24] Davis had visited Stu's father in the Etretat Hospital in 1918.

territories. At home, the cadets watched and debated news reports of the various anti-war and pro-Nazi movements. In the same way their alumni predecessors began mentally preparing for a coming war, Stu's class learned the geography, the history and military culture of possible future enemies. Most believed that the next war would be "theirs" and began preparing mentally.

By September 1939, the West Pointers were analyzing German *blitzkrieg* tactics in Poland and by the time graduation came in June 1940, German forces were already in Belgium, Luxembourg and the Netherlands and threatening France. Britain sent an Expeditionary Force to France but together, the *blitzkrieg* combination of infantry supported by tanks and aircraft was no match for the Franco-British allies and the emergency evacuation at Dunkirk was the result.

Through the summer of 1940, Stu and the other new Army Second Lieutenants followed closely the aerial Battle of Britain, German submarine predations right off the US east coast, and brutal Japanese conquests in China and Korea. President Roosevelt was taking a hard line against Japan economically and was contriving ways to support Britain with military supplies and foodstuffs.

The West Point Class of 1940 knew it was just a matter of time.

CHAPTER 15

The US Enters World War II

After Pearl Harbor was bombed by the Japanese on December 7, 1941, many National Guard units were federalized and deployed for training. The 28th Infantry Division, a part of the Pennsylvania National Guard, was among them and sent to Louisiana. Colonel Frank Rittersberg, Jr. was assigned to Headquarters of the Pennsylvania National Guard and had an additional duty assignment on the Division Staff.

Frank was just back from attending his father's funeral at West Point. The Yellow Fever that Franz Sr. had contracted during the Spanish-American War in Cuba ultimately resulted in the liver disease that led to his death at age 71. Frank's responsibilities with training the 28th Division necessitated shortening his bereavement leave. In haste, he went from West Point to Harrisburg. Unsure of what he should be doing with the family's old farmhouse, he told his father's housekeeper, Bertha, that she could live in the house rent-free, if she would continue to take care of it as she had, while his father was still living.

Early on the morning after Frank's return to Camp Livingston, Louisiana, he had just stepped out of

BEEFSTEW SAVES LIVES ON D-DAY

the shower in the VOQ[25] at, when the phone rang. A woman on the calling end said, "Please hold for General Eisenhower."

"Frank, I was so sorry to hear about your father. I wanted to be at the funeral but really couldn't be away right now. How are you holding up? Listen, I know you have your hands full with the 28th Division down there and you'll have many questions but I just asked George Marshall to recall you to active duty and I need you here in Washington Thursday. I already cleared it with Brad.[26] We'll have to talk then 'cause we can't talk on the phone. OK?"

Frank took a Pullman train to Washington's Union Station and a taxi to Army Headquarters. Ike couldn't squeeze him in till 6pm. Ike cut right to the chase.

"We are going to invade North Africa and George Marshall has named me Commander of the Allied Expeditionary Force. He agreed to let me pick my planning team. I want you to come to Gibraltar with me. How soon can you get away?"

---

[25] Visiting Officers Quarters

[26] Ike refers to Brigadier General Omar Bradley, the Commanding Officer of the 28th Infantry Division, which had been federalized from the Pennsylvnia National Guard.

CHAPTER 16

August 1942 – Chemical Warfare Research at Porton Down, UK

M iss Blake laid the morning post in the "IN" box on Dr. Charles Alton's desk. "There's one from Whitehall," she noted. "It's marked for you only and I had to sign for it." Alton, Director of the War Department Experimental Research Ground at Porton Down, said a smiling, "Thank you Carole" and reached for the large tan envelope marked "ON HIS MAJESTY'S SERVICE" and "To be opened only by Director, Dr. Charles Alton ."

Alton read the letter stamped "SECRET" twice before calling to Miss Blake, "Carole; please ask Mr. Carstairs to come and see me."

Clive Carstairs, Head of Section 3, read the letter Dr. Alton handed him:

1. The Minister of War has directed that Project 2624 (FENCEPOST) be terminated immediately as part of an earlier decision that the use of such products

would violate this country's reservations concerning chemical weapons.

2. All documents pertaining to FENCEPOST, including informal laboratory notes, will be marked SECRET and stored in secure archives.

3. All substances and products resulting from FENCEPOST experiments shall be subjected to witnessed destruction.

4. FENCEPOST staff may be immediately reassigned other work but reminded of the project's continuing SECRET classification and of their personal security obligations.

The letter was signed by Robert O'Dell, Secretary to the Chief of Staff.

Carstairs met Edward Collins, Leading Staff Chemist on Project FENCEPOST in the hallway and passed on the War Office instructions verbally. Collins had been getting bored with FENCEPOST and wasn't sorry to see it ended. A 1941 honors graduate in chemistry from Magdalene College, Cambridge, Collins eagerly accepted appointment at Porton Down and his first salaried position. A committed communist, he had conflicted views about the war and his support of the British role but was unreservedly in favor of Soviet Russia's resistance to Nazi aggression.

Very soon after starting work at Porton Down, Alf Lewis, a school chum and fellow communist from Cambridge contacted him and bought him a drink at the Earl of Normanton pub, near Collins' rooming house. Quiet conversation was difficult in the noisy pub so they drained their glasses and continued talking while strolling outside and went into the graveyard of St. Nicholas' Church, pretending to look at gravestones. Lewis was secretly feeding information to a Soviet attaché, who had made him memorize a short list of places and subjects of interest. Porton Down was on the list; would Collins be willing to help?

"Since I arrived, I've only been on the one project and it's just been sacked," Collins confided.

"Oh, what was that then?"

"FENCEPOST they called it. We were developing a highly concentrated mixture of sodium phosphate, ipecac, and other stuff that would cause violent vomiting and diarrhea for 48 hours. It was supposed to be mixed in enemy troops' rations and make them unable to fight. We developed a slow-release agent that bonded with the active ingredients, assuring that around 50% of what was ingested would pass into the small intestine so that what was ingested wouldn't be vomited out right away. But you'd have to use a lot of the stuff and we could never solve the problem of how to get it mixed in food. I think the project was cancelled 'cause it wasn't very practical."

"Interesting. I wonder if my chap at the embassy might be interested. If he wants the formula, could you give it to me?"

"Sure. I can write it out for you now. There's not much to it."

Lewis fished out a pencil and the copy of *Wiltshire Walking Paths* he had in his coat pocket and handed them to Collins. Making sure no one was watching, Collins found a page with some white space and wrote out the formula with a couple of guidance notes. Handing back the book, Collins said soberly, "Take care to completely destroy the whole book, Alfie. Not just the page with the formula."

CHAPTER 17

September 1942 - Joseph Stalin

In the late summer of 1942, the German 6th Army had crossed the border of the USSR and was pushing steadily toward Stalingrad. The Soviets threw everything they had into a desperate bid to stop the invaders' advance and staggering numbers of Red Army soldiers died in the attempt. Unsure of how long he could hold off the Germans, Stalin anxiously pressured Franklin Roosevelt and Winston Churchill to hurry along the contemplated Allied invasion of occupied France as one way to force Hitler to pull some troops off the eastern front. Anticipating that the "second front" would be opened in due time, Stalin ordered that encouragement and as much support as possible should be provided for the French communists in the anti-German *Résistance*.

In addition to urging relief from the acute pressure being brought to the Russian Motherland, Stalin kept an eye on France, which he believed would suffer at least momentary anarchy immediately following her

liberation, which Stalin knew was coming. French communists formed a major share of the *Résistance* and would be expected to fill any void with swift seizures of control and steps to delegitimize Charles de Gaulle, who had spent the war pontificating authoritatively but safely from London.

Stalin knew that the Communist members of the *Résistance* would be less likely than most of the French to relax in celebration of liberation and would be armed and ready to seize control.

The Soviet dictator and his inner circle knew clearly that a successful Allied invasion of occupied France was as important to the USSR as it was to the French. Accurate, detailed intelligence on Rommel's "Atlantic Wall" reaching Moscow painted as daunting as picture as it did in England. Reasoning that the Allied invasion *must* succeed, Stalin continually prodded his staff for information on the French communists and whether they were getting what they needed.

A serious challenge facing the Soviets was the reality that the *Résistance* was by necessity anonymous, suspicious, and tightly secretive. The Soviets were frustrated at the aggravating slowness of communications. Mail could not be used, radio was somewhat unreliable, subject to interception and jamming, and sometimes used by the Germans to locate *Résistance* members through direction finding. When radio was used, messages were drastically cut short and transmitters were cautiously "on the air" for the briefest times. Travel by couriers was slow and highly dangerous and the long distances from Soviet airfields made dropping agents into France by parachute impossible. As a workable alternative, Party leaders in

Moscow proposed inserting capable, trusted agents into the French *Résistance* with encouragement to do the best they could to support the British and Americans as the means also to help the USSR.

The Party leaders set up a clandestine postal system based on trusted couriers, sending coded and microfilmed messages, and only as much radio as could be risked. Bernard Perrier, a mathematics teacher and *Résistance* leader in the small French port city of Barfleur, had come to the attention of the Moscow leadership as one worth supporting. Since the middle of 1941, Moscow was exchanging correspondence with Perrier on microfilmed papers including letters, sketches, photographs, activity logs, and stolen German documents. However; because of the acute difficulties of secure travel, the microfilm mail route was torturously slow.

The efficient Germans used their own and captured railroads very effectively and the Soviets learned how to hide the microfilm mail on railcars where it could be retrieved by an operative, who knew where to look. The hardest part was determining the destination of a railcar and then sending the intended recipient a brief radio message with the railcar's serial number. Try as they would, the Germans could not provide complete security for long-distance trains rolling through field and forest and the anti-Germans learned to place and retrieve microfilm mail on slow moving and stopped trains.

A route that offered a low risk of interception was travel by a courier from Moscow to Poti in Soviet Georgia, home port of a Black Sea Fleet submarine squadron. A submarine would drop a courier on the Romanian coast, who would then use the German-controlled rail system with ingenuity and daring.

In November 1943, Bernard Perrier was told by a local cell member that Moscow had forwarded a microfilmed summary of British chemical warfare and engineering activities. Always open to innovative ideas, Perrier scanned the summary with a magnifying viewer for anything they might use – someday. He skimmed over the first seven British projects, concerning defensive equipment and medical treatments, without any interest. The eighth item reported that the research station at the Porton Down laboratories had terminated Project FENCEPOST, development of a highly concentrated agent causing prolonged and incapacitating vomiting and diarrhea. "Delivery impractical" was cited as the reason for termination. The agent's chemical formula and instructions were included. The ninth item on the microfilmed list asked for samples of sand from Normandy beaches.

Perrier gave the summary to Josephine Aguillon suggesting, "The last two items are interesting. See if we can find a way to use the chemical formula. And get word to Pierre Fermier that we need small samples of beach sand – about 30 millilitres."[27]

---

[27] Approximately one liquid ounce.

CHAPTER 18

1942 – France, Josephine Aguillon

Josephine Aguillon, dedicated communist and pre-occupation trade unionist, was the wife of a commercial fisherman. His trawler, BR-51, was one of the few remaining in the port of Barfleur on the Cotentin Peninsula, 20 miles east of Cherbourg. Before the Germans came, her husband, Etiennne, regularly brought back enough fish, shellfish, and lobster to provide a comfortable living and employment for three crewmen. Following France's 1940 surrender, the Germans limited his allowance of diesel fuel and restricted him to no further than ten *kilometers*[28] from shore. German patrol boats zealously enforced the restriction, ostensibly to prevent any contact with British or American vessels. Only permitted to leave port three days per week, Etienne could only pay one crewman and saw his income reduced by 40%.

Etienne chafed under the very frequent German boardings of BF-51, searching for contraband and enemy agents, who might be

---

[28] Just over six miles

attempting to enter or leave France. Invariably, boarding parties enjoyed intimidating him and his mate by pointing MP-40 submachine guns at their faces and left his boat with the biggest lobsters he had, paying for them with mocking smiles.

Until the war and German occupation, Etienne's brother Theo, had a fish market near the docks in Barfleur and sold all of Etienne's catch. But Theo was called up for Army service in 1940 and was so seriously disabled at the Battle of Stonne that he was unable to work and the store closed.

Now, Josephine and her sister-in-law Veronique, met Etienne's boat at the dock, where BR-51's catch was off-loaded into an old, rusting *Citroën* truck. The two ladies were allowed to deliver the seafood to a German Army central commissary in Valognes, 20 miles away. Lobster and sole were most wanted. German sentries at checkpoints along the road felt free to offend the women with blatant ogling, unwanted suggestions, and lewd comments among themselves in German. Josephine and Veronique felt a seething hatred for the occupiers and bided their time, awaiting the opportunity to strike back.

Bernard Perrier, teacher and *Résistance* leader in Barfleur, was dedicated to a Communist France after the hoped-for liberation, and used Josephine as a courier. Josephine's son, Alain, was one of Perrier's students. Josephine's frequent deliveries to Valognes offered opportunities to cross paths with other *Résistance* members and forward surreptitious messages by hand-signals, word-of-mouth and paper.

CHAPTER 19

1942 - *Soldat* Dieter Roeder

Dieter grew up on his family's small farm just outside Mainz. His parents, Bruno and Anna worked without stop to make do, customarily foregoing whatever wasn't really needed. Bruno farmed potatoes and winter wheat while Anna looked after chickens and kept a kitchen garden. On Market Day, Anna sold potatoes at a stall in the *Mainzer Marktplatz* [29] and bartered with other sellers for milk, cheese, and meat. Bruno was already too old for the army in 1939 and had, years before, lost his right thumb and pointing finger in a thresher accident. Life had become increasingly difficult for Bruno after his two oldest sons went into the navy. A committed Nazi sympathizer, Bruno loudly voiced his strong support of Hitler and was proud to boast of his sons at the local *bierstube*,[30] one a U-Boat sailor and the other on the Battleship Tirpitz. In Nazi Germany, no one would dare risk whispering an anti-government sentiment – especially not while Bruno Roeder might hear and report you.

The war and its supporting industrialization made it impossible to hire any farm labor and the Roeder farm

---

[29] Market Place

[30] A bar serving beer

was too small to qualify for Polish prisoners, essentially slave labor. So Bruno tried increasingly to get help from 15 year old Dieter.

At school, about which he was basically indifferent, Dieter was considered a slow learner. Easily distracted by the most mundane objects, Dieter could focus intently on a blonde hair of his forearm or an ant crawling across his desk. Years into the future, Dieter would be described as having Attention Deficit Disorder. The boy made no friends at school, was bullied and stood aside during outdoor recess, focusing on miniature objects while the others engaged in physical activities. His frustrated teachers basically gave up on him, sending him off to the next grade to be another teacher's problem.

Dieter's savvy father, knowledgeable about Nazi Aryan Purification policies, worried that Dieter might come to the attention of those who would select him for sterilization. So, rationalizing that Dieter's help was needed on the farm and that his mother could teach him at home, Bruno pulled the boy out of school.

At first, Dieter enjoyed his release from the structure and discipline of the classroom but was soon ready for release from his father's endless list of chores and day-long schedule. Although he believed himself honestly trying, Dieter could never satisfy his father in terms of finishing a task correctly or completing it on time. Whenever out of Bruno's sight, Dieter could always find pause to study the paths of dripping water running down a pole or how sunlight filtering in between barn boards made stripes across the floor. He made crude human and animal figures from strands of straw, sometimes soldiers with rifles. He was mesmerized by bird song, especially when he perceived birds answering one another. The boy received a deserved share of scoldings from his father – some laced with harsh terms of ridicule – and the occasional attention-getting kick in the behind. Bruno's long-winded verbal report card and humiliating instruction became commonplace at the dinner table with the boy and his mother eating in silence with downcast eyes. Anna held her piece but hastened to excuse and comfort Dieter after Bruno had left. A pattern took hold in which Bruno cleaned his plate and stomped out followed by Dieter getting up and going to Anna for a reassuring hug and comforting words.

On his 18th birthday in 1942, Dieter received a conscription order from the *Wehrpflichtamt* [31] in Mainz. Bruno made a personal appearance, pleading for Dieter's deferment. He cited the boy's essential farm work and the fact that his brothers were in the *Kriegsmarine*.

"Are your two sailor-sons still alive?" Bruno was asked. Bruno's "yes" response ended the interview.

"Your son must follow the instructions in the draft order."

Bruno was annoyed at having been trivialized by the *Wehrpflichtamt*. Anna was badly frightened at the prospect of sending her sensitive, immature boy off to the army and to war. Dieter had mixed emotions about being a soldier. He was uncomfortable with the notion of becoming an incarnation of his soldier-straw figure but excited to be escaping from his father's rule. The boy

---

[31] Draft Board

never considered that he might be going from the frying pan into the fire.

Anna bravely controlled her emotions at Dieter's departure but broke down in wracking sobs as Bruno drove their son and a small suitcase off the farm and onto the road to the station in Mainz.

"Be a man," Bruno urged, clapping Dieter on the back and then leaving him immediately. Bouncing in the horse-drawn wagon on the way back to the farm, Bruno's confused thoughts danced between dread that Dieter would be killed to whether he might make a good soldier to the stigmatizing possibility he would be found unfit and sent home.

Dieter did not become a good soldier. He couldn't retain knowledge of right from left. He cleaned his uniform, barracks area, and latrine assignment indifferently. He was hopeless with a rifle, loading too slowly, aiming with shaking hands as he fearfully anticipated the loud "bang" and recoil. He drew frequent punishments such as digging latrine trenches, hours of marching with a full pack, and denial of rations. Criticisms often brought him to tears and he was believed to have been heard murmuring "*Mutti*" after a sergeant's abusive dressing-down. Exasperated non-commissioned officers recommended that he be discharged but they were denied, acute manpower needs being cited.

So Dieter, found unfit for any army job, was reassigned to Army Group B in occupied Normandy as a casual laborer. He spent long hours alongside Polish slave-laborers carrying 20-kilogram bags of cement and sand. He dug foundations for beachfront bunkers and machine gun nests along Rommel's "Atlantic Wall." When the cement emplacements were dry, he filled and stacked sandbags against and atop the walls. His work was slow and his workmates soon gave up as useless trying to hurry him along. *Soldat* Roeder was earmarked as a misfit loner and, as long as he caused no disruptive trouble, was mostly ignored. He entertained himself making crude sand figures and spent many hours gazing out to sea at nothing in particular. Dieter's occasional boyish letters home gave his parents no cause for worry. Had he gone absent, his unit might have delayed reporting him.

CHAPTER 20

1943 - Yuri Gregorevich Egorov

Looking up at the night sky, the man in railway worker's grubby clothes paused partway into the hatch, took a last deep breath of fresh salty ocean air and continued down into Submarine S33, with the name "Спрут"[32] painted in white on the hull.

He was the only one boarding the S33 docked at the Poti sub base not in Soviet naval uniform, Yuri Gregorevich Egorov attracted numerous quizzical looks from crew and shore support personnel but all were savvy enough to hold their tongues.

Having made this hateful Black Sea crossing five times before, Yuri Gregorevich knew already to keep out of the way and let the crew make ready to cast off. It reminded him of the ballet as he pirouetted, ducked, and squeezed himself forward between groceries, equipment, pipes and sailors to the cramped bay where the crew slept. Gratefully, he climbed into a narrow sweat-smelling bunk and closed his eyes. In moments, he was asleep, undisturbed by shuffling feet, shouted commands and metal-on-metal clanking.

---

[32] Спрут (transliterated as "Sprut") = "Octopus"

S33 was making a repeated covert run from her USSR base to the town of Olimp on the coast of German-allied Romania. General Ion Antenescu had led a *coup d'état* that toppled Romania's neutral government and promptly declared allegiance to Hitler's Germany. As a trusted ally, Antonescu's dictatorship freed German troops from occupying Romania but Romania's secret police lacked the diligence of the *Gestapo*, leaving Romania easier to penetrate and travel without high risk.

S33's immediate mission was to arrive undetected very near the shore on a night chosen during a new moon and put Yuri Gregorevich, a GRU[33] Special Agent, ashore from an inflatable dinghy. To avoid detection by German destroyers and aircraft, the sub skipper, Commander Goluvin stayed close to the Turkish coast and surfaced only at night to charge batteries and make best speed.

On arrival at Yuri Gregorevich's getting-off point, Goluvin checked first through his periscope and then ordered S33 to surface. Two sub crewmen paddled their passenger under a derelict wooden pier they had used before and he climbed to the walkway, silently waved his thanks and went carefully ashore.

Concealed in thick bushes, the wary intruder looked and listened carefully before walking toward a former fish-processing plant and its decaying wooden picket fence. Moving to his right and

---

[33] GRU = *Glavnoye Razvedyvatel'noye Upravleniye*, the Main Intelligence Agency of the General Staff of the Soviet Armed Forces.

counting pickets, Yuri Gregorevich found the hollowed-out cache in which he hid his forged Romanian papers and, holding his breath in expectation of a searchlight and orders shouted at him, paused and then retrieved the flat packet.

Wasting no time, he headed inland through forest that he knew well, moving at a pace that would get him to the farm of Elena Petrescu before daybreak

Looking at the small farmhouse in the pre-dawn faint light, Yuri Gregorevich saw nothing suspicious and did not see the prearranged danger signal that Elena would have left as a warning not to approach. Elena had been badly frightened by his two previous arrivals as his schedule was kept secret for security reasons. She didn't know he was there now, was most likely still asleep so Yuri Gregorevich stayed silently in the trees until he saw a light go on in the kitchen followed by Elena going to the nearby outhouse. As she was retracing her steps to the house, he whistled a famous passage from a Romanian Rhapsody by George Enescu, known to all Romanians.

Elena looked at once in his direction, a broad welcoming smile brightening her old wrinkled face. Inside, they spoke very simply as Yuri Gregorevich, although fluent, pretended that his Romanian was limited. Elena suspected that he came from somewhere across the Black Sea but wasn't sure if he was a Turk, a Bulgarian, or a Russian. Studying his black hair, thick black moustache, and dark brown eyes, the old woman was curious but held back her questions. Whoever he was; they were on the same side, resisting the hated German occupiers and their Romanian Nazi allies. She never questioned him and he volunteered nothing that she would need to protect.

It was the same as his last visits: he needed only to stay one night until her old neighbor, Ion Bălan came with his horse and wagon to pick up the eggs she was sending to market in the nearby town of Mangalia. Bălan, slow and in his 70s, helped the resistance as best he could. The road to Mangalia wasn't regularly patrolled and there was no German military activity in the area so the slow trip to town didn't seem too risky.

Bălan knew only that this stranger, whose name he didn't know or ask, again wanted only to get off his egg and produce cart near the houses close to the rail yard in Mangalia. The trip was as uneventful as the previous five, conversation limited to the weather and Ion's horse until Yuri Gregorevich was off with a wave, walking calmly to the railroad dispatch office. Bălan focused on keeping to the right, not watching his former passenger walk off.

In the dispatch office, Yuri Gregorevich walked up to Constantin Vasilescu's desk and had to correct the dispatcher with slight head shaking and making a small circle with his lips. Vasilescu was surprised to see this mystery man again and almost gave him away by a startled reaction.

Remembering the drill, the dispatcher simply wrote a Train Number, a time and Track Number on a slip of paper and slid it in Yuri Gregorevich's direction. With his paper in hand, the Russian posing as a Romanian rail worker, bought two apples from the fruit stand and went out to the track where his assigned train was getting ready to leave. His clothes and features helped him look as though he belonged as he made his way past the idling locomotive, coal car, and 36 tank cars to the brake cabin[34] "Number 83" at the end of the train. Inside, he made sure there was drinking water in the small keg and took a seat.

Hearing the locomotive whistle's two long blasts, Yuri Gregorevich pulled the green flag from its holder on the wall, swung down to the ground, and waved to the engineer. As the coal-burner belched thick black smoke, he climbed back up to the brake cabin as the train slowly eased westward toward the capital city of Bucharest, where it would be switched toward the oilfields of Ploesti. Yesterday, the locomotive had pulled tank cars filled with bunkering oil for German Navy ships in port at Deveselu. Now, it would pick up another shipment in Ploesti before heading back to the port.

It was to Ploesti that Yuri Gregorevich wanted to go. His assignment sternly charged by his superior, Vladimir Alexandrovich Chernetsky was that by any means necessary, put his "parcel" on the last tank car of a train going from Ploesti to the German refinery near Hanover and to memorize the car's number painted on the tank. Making himself as comfortable as he could for the six hour clickety-clack ride, Yuri Gregorevich considered that all was going according to plan and he dozed off. The jarring stop in the railyard outside Bucharest woke him. He stood, opened the side window and poked his head out. A handful of German troops were superficially inspecting the train before allowing it to proceed to the strategically important oilfields. One middle-aged, out-of-shape NCO ambled back to the brake cabin, saw Yuri Gregorevich looking out and exchanged nods with

---

[34] Brake Cabin: equivalent to an American caboose.

him, his bored expression never leaving his face. At the two-blast signal from the locomotive whistle, Yuri Gregorevich repeated his green flag "OK" response and the train chugged onto its new northbound track.

It was nearly dark when the train reached the Ploesti rail terminal. Tomorrow, a designated crew would move the train through the filling station and manually insert the filling arm into each open tank car. When a tank car was full, the engineer would be signaled to move forward precisely far enough to fill the next car. Yuri Gregorevich walked to the Dispatcher's Building and went directly to the men's toilet and then the little café on the far side of the large room.

Having eaten nothing all day other than the two apples he bought in Mangalia, he hopefully ordered a bowl of *Ciorbă de fasole*[35] and a chunk of bread. Eating slowly from a table in the corner, he took in the postings on the walls, the few others lounging or milling about, and – most especially – no one whose appearance or demeanor revealed him to be military or security. He mopped up the last of his soup with the bread and took his bowl and spoon to the cart with dirty dishes waiting to be rolled back to the kitchen. On the wall outside the dispatcher's window, Yuri Gregorevich found the list of scheduled departures and track numbers. His return train to Mangalia would be on Track 6, departing at 4am. Three lines down, he found: "Train K64-228 to Hanover/Uetze - Track 8 at 2:40am."

Yuri Gregorevich went again into the men's toilet and entered a stall. From between the two layers of his trousers

---

[35] A Romanian bean soup.

suspenders, he pulled out a slim strip of microfilm protected by green paper. With practiced fingers, the microfilm was rolled into a mini-cylinder the size of a small nail. He then took out his little tobacco pouch and a cigarette paper. He rolled a cigarette with the microfilm at one end and sealed it by moistening one edge with his tongue. Yuri Gregorevich tucked his secret cargo above his ear and arranged his long hair to cover it. If necessary to escape detection, he could always hold the cigarette in his lips and even light the end without the microfilm.

Back at the café counter, he bought a piece of yellow *Kashkaval* cheese on a piece of coarse grey paper and a bottle of *Ursus* beer and headed back to the lines of cars waiting to be pulled out. To reach his train on Track 6, he needed to walk the length of the train on Track 8 (his target) and pass behind its brake cabin. Cautiously looking for anyone who might question him, Yuri Gregorevich stepped soundlessly to the rear of the last of the brown tank cars, took the cigarette with the mini-cylinder of microfilm from above his ear and pushed it into the lowest hollow rung of the car's metal ladder. He plugged the hollow rung with a piece of his cheese wrapper and moved away toward Track 6. In a last look back at the tank car with his microfilm, the number DRB+16314 found a place in his memory.

 Yuri Gregorevich's task completed, he got back up into the brake cabin he would ride back to Mangalia, look for Ion Bălan the egg-man, and send a radio message and sleep at Elena's farmhouse. Then he would take the long walk through the forest back to the coast to be picked up by the submarine for that rotten trip back across the Black Sea to Mother Russia. Confident he had done his duty, Yuri Gregorevich drank his beer and dozed off. He had no idea what was on the microfilm or where it was going. Neither did he know that, just outside Hanover, Jens Karloff would push the cigarette-wrapped microfilm out of the lowest hollow ladder-rung using his long-necked oil can.

The next day, after the egg-man dropped him off, Elena greeted Yuri Gregorevich at the door and spontaneously hugged him. The aged widow had come to think of him as a son, fighting for Romania's freedom and she derived satisfaction from giving him the little help she could. Elena made them both a cup of tea, apologized that she had no sugar but he pretended not to understand. He smiled without speaking and they both sat, looking appreciatively at each other. They never spoke much, his Romanian was disguised as very limited and he didn't want to speak Russian to her. So much she wanted to know about this stranger with whom she was resisting the *Oribil de Germani*[36] but she was astute enough not to ask questions. She sat quietly when he dozed off. Assuming that his work was dangerous and tense, it warmed her to be watching him protectively.

---

[36] Horrible Germans

Elena would never forgive the louts who showed up at her little chicken farm in the winter of 1940. The four, who stopped their truck at her gate, wore uniforms but didn't look like real soldiers to Elena, who kept to herself and wasn't well-informed about the political situation. They were middle-aged, slovenly, unshaven and apparently drunk. One wearing sergeant's chevrons rudely demanded to know where Elena's husband was and, when she informed him that Petru had been dead for 12 years, pushed past her into the house, the other three following.

The four immediately set to noisily searching the house. The sound of furniture being moved upstairs and things being dropped on the floor were frightening and she trembled, her apron lifted to her mouth. One of the men came down the stairs and carried her wall clock out the door. She followed one of them into her kitchen and watched him take her large kitchen knife and her husband's bottle of *Tuica* plum brandy that had sat in the cupboard untouched since his death. Elena stammered, "No" and stepped forward but the soldier shoved her roughly and she fell backward, injuring her hip. From the floor, her last sight of him was taking the pot of soup she had on the wood stove and carrying it out. The sergeant looked at her lying in pain, his left hand holding the little *Horezu*[37] vase she and Petru had bought years before as a souvenir of their anniversary trip to Bucharest. Smirking, he gave her a Nazi salute, "*Heil Antenescu si Hitler*"[38] and was out the door.

When Elena was finally able to stand and slowly climb the stairs, she discovered that all the drawers of her little

[37] A Romanian pottery brand
[38] Heil Antonescu and Hitler

dresser were dumped and scattered and her mattress was likewise on the floor. She had to sleep on the floor for five nights until Ion Bălan stopped by for eggs and helped her reassemble the bed. Her lasting souvenir of her violation was walking with a cane to ease the bruised hip that never stopped hurting. Bălan explained to her that their country was now on Germany's side in the war and that the army included many bullies and criminals.

When it was dark, Yuri Gregorevich went down into the cellar, where Elena let him hide his radio transmitter. Stowed with the radio were a telegrapher's key, a long extension cord and a coiled, very long antenna wire. Bounding up the stairs, trailing the extension cord, he went into Elena's small sitting room, where she had an electric table lamp. Once the bulb was removed, one end of the extension cord was inserted into the socket. He next went outside and loosely wound one end of the coiled antenna wire around an old rusty nail near the northeast corner of the house. Moving quickly, he reached the piece of wood siding with the end that he had earlier pried up just enough to hold the wire and then pushed the remaining coil through the open top of the small cellar window.

A quick look around as he moved to the front door revealed nothing suspicious. Without a word, Yuri Gregorevich went down to the basement, plugged-in the radio and anxiously watched for it to warm up. As before, Elena stayed upstairs keeping watch and was ready to signal with her cane on the floor – three knocks, if she saw anyone on or near her property.

With steady hands, he dialed the frequency 4435 Kilocycles[39] and when his watch read 2213 hours,[40] Yuri Gregorevich began his message using Morse code, assuming the submarine on listening watch in the Black Sea was on station and ready to receive. His message was brief, without any callsigns or tuning chatter. From memory, he recalled the number of the tank car on which he concealed the message and mentally added a "2" to each digit or letter so that "16314" became "38536," Train Number "K64-228" became "M86440." "Hanover/Uetze" was simplified to "UZ" and encoded as "XF," all of which would be understood by his GRU comrades at headquarters. Sending his dots and dashes deliberately at about 15 words per minute, the message he transmitted was:

38536 M8644 0XF

He was "off the air" as quickly as possible, hoping the German *Sicherheitsdienst*[41] would not detect his transmitter on the one-time use frequency and that it would not be necessary for him to retransmit in ten minutes. His brief wait was tense; he didn't want the risk of a retransmission. In exactly 30 seconds after he stopped sending, he was relieved to hear an acknowledgement as simply a three-second solid tone, sent twice and exhaled.

Understanding that a radio operator on the submarine had received his message and would relay it to the GRU, Yuri Gregorevich dismantled his makeshift sending station

---

[39] In the high frequency band. "Kilocycles" is an archaic term now replaced by Kilohertz (KHz).

[40] 10:13pm

[41] Security Service, which listened for enemy radio signals.

and hid the components. He bade farewell to Elena in Romanian, "*Adio*" and pressed a thin gold ring into her hand. She hugged him tightly, returning his "*Adio Băiatul meu. Sper să te văd din nou*"[42] and watched him walk into the woods in the direction of the old fish processing plant.

He hid his Romanian papers with the forged German rubber stamps in the decaying wooden picket fence of the old fish-processing plant. For safety, Yuri Gregorevich spent the next several hours in the woods, keeping a watch on the rotting wooden pier where the sub's inflatable would pick him up at 0300[43] hours.

108

CHAPTER 21

Pierre Fermier, The Trashman

From habit, Leo the brown horse stopped at the guard shack barrier at the entrance to 726 Grenadier Regiment's forward defensive positions overlooking a stretch of sandy beach that would come to be forever known as "Omaha." A German guard recognized Leo and his driver, Pierre Fermier, and raised the barrier. The guard had left his *Mauser Karabiner* rifle leaning against the shack and he turned his face away as Leo pulled the garbage wagon through without being inspected. The smell was sickening and the flies were worse.

The Germans had given Pierre Fermier the job of collecting garbage placed in cans outside the bunkers and artillery casemates. The twice-per-week routine was unchanging: Leo walked slowly among the rough concrete structures as Pierre lifted and dumped the cans into the wagon. On some days, a young German *soldat* came up to Leo, fed him a saved piece of apple and affectionately stroked his nose. Leo reminded Dieter Roeder of the farm horse, Heinie, at home.

But Pierre was more than a trashman. Old and unkempt, reeking of garbage, Pierre was an unlikely member of the *Résistance*. Clomping around in his time-worn shoes that now had wooden soles, he seemed a most unlikely threat to German secrets. Valued for his clearance to enter German military facilities and his keen eye for detail and sharp memory, Pierre reported his observations to a man he knew only by the *nom de guerre*, Pelléas. When he had something to report, Pierre hung a bucket from the left rear corner of the wagon; if there was nothing to report, the bucket hung from the right rear corner. As Leo clopped his way to the town dump, fellow *Résistance* member, Pelléas, watched for the signal to meet Pierre at Leo's paddock in *Vierville sur Mer* that night where he committed to his memory what Pierre retrieved from his own.

Among the bits of information noted by Pierre Fermier that had found their way into the agent's report transmissions:

- The Field Post Number of the infantry unit at *Colville-sur-Mer* is 19930/C (this from a Postal Cover from *Familie* Bergdorf to *Sold.* E. Bergdorf and recovered from trash Fermier collected).
- Fortifications along the seawall at *Colville-sur-Mer* are being made from cement mixed with beach sand.
- FPN 19930/C is practicing timed relocation from shelter to action stations (this from Fermier's observation on his successive collection days of

troops emerging from bunkers at the run carrying machine guns and boxes while NCOs screamed "faster" at them).

- During some timed practices, machine guns were fired at large wooden targets floating very close to shore.
- FPN 19930/C is well-provisioned, with no apparent food shortages (this from Fermier's report that edibles were being routinely thrown out).

As soon as he was back in his own house, Pelléas wrote down the garbage man's observations in a pre-arranged code, minimizing his words and writing in tiny block letters on small pieces of  cigarette paper. He next rolled the paper and inserted it into a miniature sleeve designed to be clipped to a pigeon's leg. At 3:00am, Pelléas cautiously stole out of the house to a shed, where he kept messenger pigeons.

Moving quickly, he clipped on the sleeve and tossed the bird, which immediately took wing toward the Channel coast. Satisfied that his message was away and that Germans with shotguns probably wouldn't see the pigeon in the dark, Pelléas went to bed. His last thoughts before sleep were mentally reviewing that he hadn't left any writing to be discovered, in the event of a search.

The pigeon, which had successfully crossed the Channel four times earlier, acquired smells it had learned and flew unerringly to its home roost on a farm just outside the village of Niton on the Isle of Wight. In the morning,

Brenda Draper noticed the arrival and retrieved the sleeve from the pigeon's leg and took it to a Royal Navy station at nearby Ventnor from where it was sent with other dispatches by motorcycle rider to London.

One rainy, windy morning, Fermier stopped Leo where Dieter Roeder had just dumped a bucket of beach sand onto the pile he had been making since after breakfast. While Dieter was petting Leo's neck, Fermier concealed an empty matchbox in his palm and let it fall next to the sand pile as he was emptying a can into the cart. The Trashman calmly picked up the match box, sliding it along the sand pile and putting it in the cart where he would be able to find it later. He had just collected 30 millilitres of beach sand that would be flown via pigeon to England for analysis.

CHAPTER 22

1943 - Ukrainians in German Uniforms

I n August 1941, the German 6th Army encircled the Ukrainian capital city of Kiev and all but annihilated defending Soviet troops, who suffered over 600,000 casualties. Many Ukrainians welcomed the Germans as "liberators" from harsh Soviet rule. During this period, the independent Ukrainian People's Army (UPA) was simultaneously anti-German and anti-USSR in its quest for sovereign statehood. Sergeant Bohdan Glushenko's UPA unit surrendered to the Germans, who believed that the anti-Soviet Ukrainians could be absorbed into the *Heer*.[44] A great many Ukrainians donned German uniforms and were shipped west, away from their home country, to serve in non-combat roles, freeing other Germans for reassignment.

Glushenko's interrogation revealed him to be a Morse radio operator and he was posted to Normandy with the 726th Infantry Division, which formed an "*Ost*"[45] Battalion with 439 of his turn-coat countrymen. After demonstrating ability to copy Morse Code at 21 words per minute, he

---

[44] German Army

[45] "East"

was assigned to the Radio Section of *Hauptman*[46] Hans Becker's Administrative and Communications Section, working on Midnight Shift.

Oberfeldwebel[47] Rolf Starke was glad to have a non-German, who would accept assignment to "straight-midnights" without whining and constantly begging for a day job. Starke warned Glushenko, "If you don't want me to shoot you personally, strictly follow three rules: One – Be at your radio position and awake at all times during your shift. Don't go for a break without permission and a replacement to guard your receiver. Two - You will only receive incoming traffic and only send to the transmitting operator what is necessary for good reception. You are not here to send official messages. Three – stay far away from the *Enigma*[48] machine and all *Enigma* key papers. Don't be caught trying to see the machines and don't ask the *Enigma* clerks any questions. Understood?

What Glushenko's interrogation didn't reveal was that he was an undercover Soviet GRU[49] agent, who had been planted in the UPA. Shortly after arriving in Normandy, he discovered a small handwritten note tucked in his straight razor in his room in the *Hôtel des Deux Poissons* in Formigny, three miles from the beach. The note read, "Maximus wants to talk." He had expected to be contacted by the GRU sooner-or-later, once they learned where he was.

---

[46] Captain

[47] Master Sergeant

[48] Cipher machine

[49] *Glavnoye Razvedyvatel'noye Upravleniye,* the Main Intelligence Agency of the General Staff of the Soviet Armed Forces.

Walking in the small town of Formigny, Glushenko was careful to avoid eye contact with strangers. His uniform bore the "YBB"[50] patch of Ukrainian "volunteers" and he cautiously regarded everyone he saw as a potential *Gestapo*[51] agent, watching  him. He used shop windows as mirrors to see what was going on behind him and left and right up the street. For two full days, no contact.

On the afternoon of the third day, Glushenko went to the open-air market to buy some grapes for his midnight duty. He noticed a German soldier wearing a Coast Artillery patch, who was also looking at grapes. Without looking at Glushenko, the soldier briefly removed his uniform cap, smoothed his hair and replaced the cap. Glushenko responded to this challenge by taking out his wallet and counting his paper money. His challenger next walked past Glushenko exactly seventeen steps, turned about and walked past Glushenko out of the market square and around the corner. Glushenko waited the specified four minutes, during which he bought a small bunch of grapes, and then followed his authenticated contact. Around the corner, he spotted the soldier crossing the street and touching the lamp post with his right hand – all fingers extended. The soldier entered a café shortly followed by Glushenko. The soldier ordered two Dubonnet aperitifs, pretended to remove a floating speck, and then drained the small glass in one gulp – the last part of the authentication ritual. This was Maximus.

---

[50] Actually Cyrillic abbreviation for *"Ukrainske Vyzvolne Viysko"* (Ukrainian Liberation Army).

[51] Secret Police

The GRU task for Glushenko was to listen for messages sent by their operatives on the same frequencies used by the German Army. Messages would be sent in the wee hours between 0300 and 0400 during lulls in network activity. Maximus told Glushenko that the German callsigns and radio net procedures were known and that the GRU would intrude messages disguised to look like *Enigma*-enciphered traffic. Glushenko was to listen for his sender's expected callsign, followed by a group of three "Vs" sent twice and then his own station's callsign and the procedure signal, "QRL IMI."[52]

"You are to reply with your station's callsign and the procedure signals, "HH QRV QRU."[53] "Copy the coded messages carefully and bring them out of the Radio Room. Maximus described a "dead drop" under a stone windowsill at the back of the former flower shop on *Rue Capet.* "The window with the white curtain hanging outside. I will know when you have left something for me, if you leave an empty pack of *Gauloises* on the reception counter of your hotel, after asking what will be served for dinner?" Your first messages for me will start on your shift tomorrow. Usually no more than two per week, never two on the same night."

Glushenko was ready. Next night at 0313 hours, he heard the callsign of his usual radio link contact on frequency 5455 kilocycles:

T6RN   T6RN   V V V   V V V   BKT8   QRL   IMI

Glushenko answered:

---

[52] QRL = "Are you busy?"

[53] HH = "Heil Hitler;" QRV = "I am ready;" QRU = "I have nothing for you."

BKT8 HH QRV QRU

Bogus Station T6RN then transmitted the message, in five-letter groups, mimicking German Army Enigma-enciphered traffic:

**PHRES MHGBV APIKD PDERD UHOVL
TWDSJ CRNJO WDQON HIGFC RSHOL
NHMNB TYMTE HH**

The bogus station, in the USSR north of Moscow was on the air for less than a minute.

Per Maximus' instructions, Glushenko hid the message he had copied in the dead-drop windowsill, left the empty *Gauloises* cigarettes packet at the hotel front desk, and asked about the dinner menu. Behind the counter, Victor Couillard excused himself and said he would ask in the kitchen. He told Sophie Millot that a soldier from the Ukrainian unit was asking about dinner and she understood there was a message at the back of the old flower shop.

"Tell him liver and onions." Hearing the expected response, Glushenko went back onto the street.

Later, Sophie retrieved the message from under the windowsill with the ragged white curtain and hid it. She told *Feldwebel*[54] Lehmann, the Mess Sergeant that she needed onions, cabbage and potatoes from the commissary at Valognes. Lehmann gave her a small truck and driver. At Valognes, Sophie slipped the message to Josephine Aguillon, who smuggled it to Bernard Perrier in Barfleur.

---

[54] Sergeant

CHAPTER 23

February 4, 1944, Chateau La Roche Guyon

T he senior officers attending the monthly program review meetings at *Chateau La Roche Guyon* usually scheduled their arrivals from deployed positions near the coast before noon. The *Feldmarschall* demanded strict punctuality and attendees were expected to be seated at the huge conference table by 1300 hours,[55] allowing ample time for travel. Besides, the sumptuous pre-conference lunch with colleagues at the imposing chateau, 40 miles north of Paris, was worth making the earlier start.

Chateau La Roche Guyon

As the antique hallway clock struck "one," *Feldmarschall* Erwin Rommel entered the room and bade his officers to sit. After brief pleasantries and good-natured ribbing of one who had broken an ankle and was on crutches, Rommel gestured to an aide, *Oberstleutenant*[56] Otto Haenchen, who reviewed the afternoon's agenda neatly written on a large sheet of paper taped to a wall.

---

[55] 1pm

[56] Lieutenant Colonel

Acting as a Master of Ceremonies, Haenchen called successive officers to stand and brief the assembled staff on construction progress, supply levels, manpower, training progress, recent Allied air strikes and overflights, and long-range weather prospects. Last on the agenda was *Oberst*[57] Anton Staubwasser, Rommel's Chief of Intelligence.

Observing that he was just back from Berlin at the quarterly intelligence review hosted jointly by the *Abwehr und Sichersheitdienst*[58], Staubwasser began, "For us in Army Group B, the most important section of the Berlin review was the Intelligence Estimate of Cross-Channel Invasion Possibilities."

Nodding in the direction of a young officer at the door, Staubwasser continued, "I have brought back important information to guide your preparations and training."

Two enlisted soldiers carried in a large white cardboard marked *"Streng Geheim"*[59] at the top and leaned it against a wall. Even before Staubwasser began to address the neatly printed information, muted gasps and whispers arose from the men at the table. Rommel loudly slapped the table wordlessly ordering "silence" and Staubwasser started through the estimate, cautioning that no notes should be taken and carried from the room.

---

[57] *Oberst: Colonel*

[58] Military Intelligence and Security Service

[59] *Streng Geheim: Top Secret*

Using a long white pointer, Staubwasser went through the list, reading each line aloud without any comment:

"Allied Forces in England:

- Ground Forces
  - Under Bradley – 90,000
  - First US Army Group under Patton – 120,000
  - British and Canadian under Montgomery – 85,000
  - French and others - 1200
  - Tanks (all countries) - 750
- Airborne Troops (*Fallschirmjaeger*[60]) – 10,000
- Naval Forces (all countries combined)
  - Landing Craft – over 4000
  - Troopships - 865"

Staubwasser paused and elaborated about the estimates for infantry, troopships, and landing craft. "Berlin believes that the Allies are nearing their target goal of troopships in English ports as few have been reported sailing from US Atlantic ports in the last two weeks. Berlin believes that infantry arriving in England will be given at least four weeks of training prior to adding them to an invasion force. Our agents in England have a highest priority watch on infantry movements from base camps to ports. The invasion should be expected within 48 hours of the first infantry troops embarking on troopships."

Staubwasser continued with the Naval Forces estimate:

- "Destroyers - 41
- Cruisers - 7
- Battleships – 11
- Minesweepers - 37

---

[60] Parachutists

- Air Forces (all countries combined)
  - Troop Carriers - 1900
  - Gliders – 600 capable of carrying 1200 troops
  - Fighter-Bombers and Long-Range Bombers – 12,000

"*Meinen herren* [61], Berlin concludes that the Allies will attempt a major invasion between now and 3 September, after which agreeable weather and a tolerable sea state may be impossible to predict with any degree of accuracy." Staubwasser continued, "Berlin expects with highest probability that infantry and tanks will be brought to beaches between Dunkirk and Boulogne but cautions that early diversionary landings may be made on *Normandie* beaches in hopes of drawing our *Panzers*[62] away from the main landing zone."

At the word "diversionary," General Erich Marcks, Commander of the 84th Korps defending Normandy, twisted sharply in his chair toward Rommel at the end of the table, accidentally knocking his cane from the back of his chair to clatter loudly on the polished marble floor and drawing a curious look from everyone in the room. General Gunther Blumentritt, sitting next to him, jumped up and retrieved the cane, rehanging it on the back of Marck's chair. The momentary distraction of the falling cane allowed Rommel to preëmpt what he knew was going to be Marck's well-known passionate dissent. "*Mein lieber Marcks,*"[63] a smiling Rommel admonished, "Let us permit *Oberst* Staubwasser to complete the

---

[61] Gentlemen

[62] Tanks

[63] My dear Marcks

presentation of the Berlin estimate. I promise you time during our discussion period."[64]

"*Danke Herr Feldmarschal*," Staubwasser said with a brief bow of his head toward Rommel and continued.

"The higher probability of the enemy's choice of the Dunkirk-Boulogne sector is seen from three important factors:

"First, we know that large ground forces need timely and rapid resupply of materiel and replacement troops. Access to a deep-water port would be critical and the logical choices are limited to Cherbourg or the trio of Calais plus Dieppe plus Le Havre. Trips across the Channel to the Normandy beaches would take four times as long as trips to the Calais sector. Also, let us not forget that the British and Canadians tried to seize Dieppe three years ago and probably still want it. The coast between Tardinghen and *Festung*[65] Philippe is the highest probability invasion point."

---

[64] Actually, Rommel did consider the Normandy coast as a likely Allied landing objective He ordered construction of defensive strongpoints as a continuation of his "Atlantic Wall." Rommel also ordered, mines and anti-tank obstacles on the beaches to prevent landing craft from coming ashore at low tide and to deny invading tanks easy passage over the beaches. Expecting the Allies to land at high tide so that the infantry would spend less time exposed on the beach, Rommel had some of the obstacles placed at the high-tide mark. Barbed wire and clearing the beach of any vegetation that offered concealment added to an invader's challenges.

[65] Staubwasser uses the German word for "fort" in mentioning the French town of Fort Philippe.

"Second, the terrain features of the Calais-area beaches feature much lower natural seawalls and bluffs. Enemy planners would interpret that as advantageous."

"And finally, the American First Army Group under Patton has grown to become one of the largest formations in England. Headquartered in Dover, Patton is America's most aggressive general and a logical choice to lead an invasion. Dover is a likely port for launching a seaborne invasion and we have reports of road-widening and staging large numbers of tanks and trucks close to the docks."

"Berlin has studied American amphibious landings in both Europe and the Far East since last year and has identified key patterns that may help us prepare for an enemy cross-Channel attempt. Some of these are obvious but are worthy of our consideration because the Allies will have no other choices."

"We can be certain that the enemy is aware from airborne photo-reconnaissance of the many obstacles we have deployed thickly along the entire northern coast of France. They will know that their only chance for troops and tanks to gain the beach is to arrive at the highest tide and in daylight. Of course, the highest tides occur around full and new moons."[66]

"A sustained naval bombardment from offshore by ships with the largest caliber guns may precede attempted landings by as much as 48 hours. Heavy bombers also may target our forward positions with many tons of

---

[66] Actually, Operation Overlord D-Day was planned for a full moon to allow aircrews (bombers, troop carriers, gliders) to see terrain features below at night.

bombs during a scheduled shelling pause after which naval guns may resume firing. Both bombing and offshore bombardment will require daylight so that must be factored into planned alerts and orders to battle stations."

Staubwasser paused and digressed, "During a prolonged heavy bombardment, the task before our men in forward positions along beaches will be simple: remain calmly within their *gruppenständ*[67] shelters, ready for the order to go to battle stations confident in the knowledge that, during bombardment, no landing craft can reach the beach and no enemy troops will yet be ashore. Officers and sergeants must reassure their men – most especially those without combat experience – that when they are ordered 'Out!' the heavy bombing and shelling will have stopped but they must move quickly and efficiently to be ready to engage targets as they come within range.

Staubwasser continued, "Berlin stresses that a period of twenty to thirty minutes normally separates the lifting of the barrage and arrival at water's edge by landing craft that will have been approaching while shells are still hitting beach defenses." Staubwasser took a step toward his seated audience and spoke slowly and authoritatively, making eye contact up and down the table, lightly pounding his left palm with his right fist: "It is critically important that commanders must obtain correct information on the approach of landing craft in their assigned sectors and not act impulsively on a bombardment pause intended to draw us out in the open, only to be exposed to a resumption of offshore shelling."

---

[67] Steel-reinforced concrete bunkers, built into land-side slopes of beachfront bluffs and designed to withstand heavy bombing and shelling.

Staubwasser pulled a large calendar from behind the large board he had been using and taped it high enough for all to see.

HIGHEST TIDES	
Full Moon	New Moon
8 - 11 March	22 - 25 March
7 - 9 April	21 - 24 April
7-9 May	21 - 24 May
5 - 7 June	19 - 21June
5 - 7 July	19 - 21July
3 - 5 August	17 - 20 August
1 - 3 September	15 - 17 September
1 - 3 October	15 - 17 October

With arms outstretched, palms turned upward, Staubwasser suggested in a facetious tone, "If they aren't here by the end of October, maybe they won't come till Spring next year. We would be better prepared by then but we must be ready for them this spring."

Generalleutnant[68] Wilhelm Richter, Commander of the 716th Infantry Division based in the town of *La Folie-Couvrechef*, just north of Caen, was tight-jawed. Staubwasser's light-hearted comment was lost on him as he contemplated the enormity of the Allied forces very possibly headed his way. In total agreement with his boss, General Marcks, Richter was impatient with the "experts," who insisted that the main thrust of the coming invasion must be at the *Pas de Calais* – the shortest cross-Channel route. Richter sensed that he needed to be as well-prepared as he could

---

[68] Lieutenant General

for major landing attempts in Normandy. He resolved to continue making those preparations and knew he had the full backing of General Marcks, if for no other reason than to avoid the appearance of softer defenses and thereby invite a major landing.

After Richter's passionate recommendations, Marcks had directed – on his own authority – construction of additional fortified machine gun nests and mortar pits along the bluff overlooking the beach to fill the gaps between the already-constructed strong bunkers. The additional nests were horseshoe shaped, open at the land side, with a ledge on the

General Erich Marcks

inside wall for machine gunners and riflemen to stand for a view of the beach and surf.

As the conference attendees at *Chateau La Roche Guyon* were heading to the driveway and their cars, Marcks pulled Richter aside and asked if he grasped the gravity of the situation. Assured that he did, Marcks asked, "Is there anything I can get you?" Now his turn for facetiousness, Richter answered, "Double everything I have now, double everything already on the way to me, and time. More time."

Marcks then made his way over to where a jovial Rommel was sharing a joke with a small circle of chuckling officers. As Marcks approached, his cane tapping the floor with each second step, the group saw his impatient, serious expression and knew he would interrupt their discussion. Rommel turned to Marcks and the others clicked their heels and left.

"Herr Feldmarshall, Staubwasser's numbers have me very concerned. I particularly noted the enemy airborne forces – 1900 Dakota troop transports, 600 gliders, and 10,000 paratroopers. And these are the 82nd and 101st Divisions – the best they have. We know that paratroopers and infantry in gliders must be transported at low altitude. Above 2500 meters[69], oxygen is required. So they must stay low but where are they going? They are not so dumb as to think of dropping on the beaches with all of our obstacles and firepower pointed at the surf. I would drop paratroops behind our beach defenses to attack from a less fortified approach. I think we will have a serious problem, if they do drop paratroops just behind the beaches at night."

"What do you suggest?"

"Herr Feldmarshall, we need mobile anti-aircraft batteries up close to the beaches – close enough so they can move quickly to fighting positions when any offshore naval shelling has stopped. I am afraid that any fixed *Flak*[70] batteries would be at risk since they must be open to the sky and can have no reinforced roofing.

"Marcks, remember, Berlin wants us to prioritize defenses in the Pas de Calais area and absolutely forbids withdrawing assets to *Normandie.*"

"Herr Feldmarshall, I must insist! Much is at stake here! I urgently recommend that you increase defenses against low-flying aircraft in our zone."

"Sehr gut [71]. I will see what I can do."

---

[69] Approximately 8000 feet

[70] Anti-aircraft

[71] Agreed

Three Days Later

A motorcycle courier brought an envelope stamped *"Geheim"*[72] and addressed to General E. Marcks at his headquarters. Inside was a copy of the Movement Order repositioning *Flakregiment* 32 of the *Luftwaffe III Flak-Korps* to wooded areas two to three miles inland from the beaches. Making the move were 32 mobile 20mm and 24 mobile 37mm anti-aircraft guns. A handwritten note signed by Rommel stated simply that he had also requested additional *Flak* support in the area of the mouth of the Orne River but that was not yet approved. He didn't tell Marcks that, with the emphasis on the *Pass de Calais*, no additional mobile units were to be moved across the Orne River, where they could become isolated, if any of the very few bridges were destroyed, making them unable to return toward Calais.

General Marcks felt reassured and went back to what he had been doing.

---

[72] Secret

Command Post, 716th *Infanterie Division, La Folie-Couvrechef, Normandie*

Generalleutenant Richter wasted no time. He called his own conference of his staff and subordinate regimental commanders and led an informal discussion of unit readiness and supply levels. He then summarized the key points from the meeting at Rommel's headquarters and emphatically issued three orders:

"Until it is positively confirmed that enemy landing craft are approaching the beach, troops will remain inside bunkers with all weapons and ammunition until ordered to battle stations." He added, "We cannot afford to lose any equipment to offshore naval artillery."

"Second, all fighting positions must be fully manned with all weapons ready within fifteen minutes of the 'Battle Stations' order. Practice realistically and repeatedly getting quickly to battle stations and assembling weapons."

"And until further notice, all units will be fully manned three days before and three days after the full and new moons . . . I will give you the dates. No leaves or passes, no absences for training during those dates when the tides will be highest. Also, plan carefully so that support staff do not need to go out of *kaserne*[73] areas to get supplies."

In turn, very sober regimental commanders repeated the division commander's orders to their subordinates and stressed that readiness training was to be stepped-up and continued until advised otherward.

---

[73] Garrison area

Oberst[74] Walter Korfes, Commander of Grenadier-Regiment 726 paid a surprise inspection visit to his 3rd Company's bunkers and defense works overlooking the beach at *Vierville*, near *Colville-sur-Mer*. As Korfes was getting out of his *Kübelwagen*,[75] he was greeted by Company Commander, *Leutenant* Edmund Bauch. The two looked at the recently-constructed Defense Works 60 and 61. Feeling the still-damp cement with his finger, Korfes remarked, "Things are coming along. When will you finish Number 62?"

"If the cement arrives on time, no more than three days," Bauch predicted, pointing to a pile of sand recently hauled from the beach in buckets by *Soldat* Dieter Roeder. "We have all the sand we can use; all we need is the cement."

"Tell me right away if there is a problem getting the cement," Korfes directed as he got into the *Kübelwagen* for the ride back to his command post in the grand 14th century *Château de Sully*.

Château de Sully

---

[74] Colonel

[75] A light 4 or 5-passenger vehicle, similar to a Jeep

Neither was aware that British commandos had recently crept ashore on the beach right in front of where they were standing to collect sand samples for analysis back in England. That analyisis sought to determine the suitability of beaches to support the weight of tanks.

CHAPTER 24

October 1943 – in Algeria

Back on active duty, Colonel Frank Rittersberg, Jr. (Stu's father) was a member of General Eisenhower's combined planning staff in Gibraltar. The Allied staff planned the invasion of North Africa, including landings in Morocco and Algeria. Frank accompanied Ike when he crossed the Mediterranean to North Africa and continued as an advisor during successful infantry and armored operations against German forces under Field Marshal Rommel.

Early one morning, Frank had been called to Ike's office in the grand old St. George Hotel in Algiers. "Frank, things are firmly on track for finishing-up here in North Africa and Italy. The President wants me back in London to run the planning for an invasion of France. I thought surely that job was going to go to George Marshall but, apparently, FDR wants to keep George in Washington. I want you and Dutch Cota to go to London and be sure the headquarters is properly staffed and headed in the right direction. I

1942: Ike in N. Africa

will disengage here as soon as I can turn things over but I might not get there till the end of the year."

Frank and Dutch Cota flew out to Lisbon, Portugal in a B-17 bomber, fitted-out as a transport and then continued on to England, giving wide berth to German-occupied France. It was a long, tedious trip with plenty of time for discussion.

Illustration of PSP usage

"Dutch, the old Tanker in me thinks I re-learned some lessons in Africa. Anywhere we plan to invade in France will need a beach and, if we are going to land tanks with the infantry, we need to make certain that the sand will support their weight. We will probably need PSP[76] for trucks and towed artillery. When we get to London, let's see what data we have on French beaches."

"Right on, Frank. That's gotta be a high priority."

---

[76] Pierced Steel Planking, commonly-used interlocking plates for providing strong weight-bearing surfaces on otherwise soft ground.

CHAPTER 25

Leutnant[77] **Edmund Bauch**

C ompany Commander Bauch, of the 726th Grenadier Regiment, was from Lindau on the north shore of the Bodensee, on Germany's border with Switzerland. Bauch had spent eighteen months with German occupation forces in Norway before being assigned to Normandy. He had been aware, since 1943, that British and American bombers were regularly raiding strategic targets in Germany and empathized with those of his men and fellow officers, who received sad news from home. The fighting had not yet reached Lindau and Bauch felt grateful but just a little bit guilty that he had no worrying news from his family.

Le Mont St Michel

Thoroughly charmed by France and all things French, *der Leutnant* was really enjoying his assignment and living in little *Vierville sur Mer*. Frequent indulgence refined his preferences for vintage Champagne, Cognac, Brie, and Roquefort. Bauch developed a nose for *Côtes*

---

[77] Lieutenant

du Rhône wines. He bought a small Citroën and played tourist in the area's cathedral towns and was especially captivated by nearby *Le Mont St Michel*, which he visited several times.[78]

Bauch's only complaint was about French coffee and often complained lightheartedly to Sophie and Cécile, cooks at the *Hôtel de la Plage,* that they should learn how brew coffee German-style.

Standing in one of his company's newly-finished mortar pits, his hands gripping the top of the semi-circular concrete wall, looking out at the English Channel, Bauch swelled with pride at German military accomplishments, at being a part of the world's strongest institution. His fingers sensed the power of Rommel's "Atlantic Wall." and assured himself that, if the Allies ever did try to storm the beaches in front of him, he would be a part of German power and that the invaders would surely fail. He believed the defenses that he and his Grenadiers manned would convince the Allies that invasion would be futile and that he would be able to enjoy his continued *séjour* [79] in France. "*Ja,* life is good, *Frankreich* [80] is sweet but so much better under German rule." Bauch hoped to stay in France for a long, long time.

Bauch didn't permit his awareness of deportations of Jews, thefts of French art, conscription of forced laborers, or summary executions of *Résistance* members spoil his enjoyment of France. He was, however, annoyed by the

---

[78] *Le Mont St Michel was not occupied by German troops. From 1940 till June 1944, great numbers of German soldiers visited.*

[79] A stay

[80] "France," in German

arrogant behavior of *SS* troops on off-duty visits to the coast, who tried to intimidate his sentries and force their way into Company 2's Restricted Zone so they could take tourist photos. When Bauch interceded and supported his sentries, one of the SS men, a *Sturmbannführer*[81] whipped out a pencil and small notebook, interrogating Bauch officiously.

Bauch stood his ground. "*Herr Sturmbannführer*, you have entered a Restricted Zone without official permission. I must ask you to leave at once or I must report this security breach to *Generalleutnant*[82] Richter, Commander of the 716th Infantry Division."

The SS officer sniffed derisively, beckoned his companions by inclining his head toward *Boulevard Cauvigny* and left. Bauch never liked the SS after that incident but worried about reprisals.

---

[81] Equivalent to Major
[82] Lieutenant General

CHAPTER 26

January 1944 – A Normandy Beach, Battle Station Drill

They had run the drill twice that morning in the cold drizzle with *Feldwebel*[83] Kellermann shrieking at them, *"Schneller! Schneller!"*[84] Now they would do it again. Kellermann made sure they stowed all the gear in the bunker's "Readiness" racks – no cheating to shave off precious seconds by having everything they would carry already in hand.

Gefreiter[85] Klaus Hammer was the crew leader of a three-man MG-42 Machine Gun crew. Hammer fired the gun, mounted on a *Lafette* 42 tripod, while *Obersoldat*[86] Rolf Emmerich fed the belts of 7.92mm ammunition. Dieter Roeder was the third crewmember. When the bell in the bunker sounded, "Battle Stations," his job was to take down the tripod from its wall mount and carry it to the gun firing position in one of the horseshoe-shaped machine gun nests 75 meters to the right of Bunker Number 60. The choreography was straightforward: the

---

[83] Feldwebel = Sergeant
[84] Faster! Faster!
[85] *Gefrieter = Corporal*
[86] *Obersoldat = Private First Class*

tripod must arrive and be properly placed on its shelf before the machine gun arrived. Anyone familiar with the operations of an MG-42 crew would know instinctively that Roeder had the easiest, least technical task.

The tripod weighed 45 pounds on its own and had been especially procured for Atlantic Wall defenses with the *Tiefenfeuerautomat* feature. This feature contributed to the gunner's accuracy by mechanically controlling the gun's tendency to recoil upward with each bullet fired.

In the first drill of the morning, Roemer forgot to lift the tripod off the wall hooks and struggled, instead, for ten seconds trying to pull it free. Not until Emmerich yelled at him to lift it did he finally get the tripod down. Next, Roeder had to angle the device, which was too wide to pass straightway through the exit door. He didn't and several more seconds were lost as both Hammer and Emmerich waiting behind him impatiently, shouted at him.

"*Nein, nein, nein!*,"[87] bellowed *Feldwebel* Kellermann. "Do it again!" During the rerun, Roeder scraped all four fingers of his right hand on the concrete doorframe and the pain made him drop the tripod. In trying to catch it before it hit the ground, the clumsy private stepped into the device's legs and fell with it, now scraping a knee.

"You dumb ass!" Hammer hissed at him. "I ought to shoot you right now."

---

[87] No, no, no!

Roeder finally put the tripod in place. His duty included returning immediately to the bunker for two hanging belts of ammunition and two boxes of belts to be brought out to Hammer and Emmerich but, going nowhere, he looked at his scraped fingers and bloody knee, feeling very sorry for himself and wanting his mother.

For the third repeat, Hammer anticipated the buzzer and stood directly behind Roemer. He talked Roemer, now wet with perspiration, through taking the tripod down and angling it through the doorway. Right behind him, Hammer thought Roemer should be moving faster but they got the gun set on the tripod in their best time of the day.

Later, Hammer discussed with *Feldwebel* Kellermann the problem he was having with Roemer. "I don't know what else I can do," Hammer confessed. "When the enemy is coming, I can't stand behind him all day waiting for the bell."

"I will have a word with him," Kellermann promised.

Later, Kellermann dragged Roemer by the scruff of his neck into a storage building, closed the door and coarsely chewed him out. He screamed, using all kinds of abusive terms: "*Dummkopf,*[88] *Ungeschicte Esel,*[89] *Nutzlosen Müll*[90] while roughing him up, shaking the cowering boy and knocking him off his feet. As Roeder was trying to get up off his hands and knees, Kellermann kicked him solidly in the pants, sending him sprawling on his face.

---

[88] Dummy
[89] Oafish donkey
[90] Useless garbage

141

"You better get it right tomorrow," Kellermann warned. "Otherwise you will wish you hadn't been born. No dinner for you tonight." Kellermann left muttering to himself and loudly slammed the door behind him.

Young Roemer sobbed as he felt the pain in his fingers, knee, buttocks, and nose, which had hit the floor after the kick. He scuttled to sit against a stack of boxes, unsure of whether he was allowed to leave. Weeping silently, he longed to be with his mother.

CHAPTER 27

January 1944 - Stu's Planning Assignment

Stu's father would never reveal to his son what very high-level strings he pulled to get him an assignment on the SHAEF planning staff that kept him in England instead of being sent Stateside. Still unhappy about being grounded but relieved to be staying in England with a role to play, Stu reported to his new job at Camp Griffiss in Bushy Park, just west of London.

Stu found his way to Hut 54 and was escorted inside to the very small office of Lieutenant Commander George Christenson, US Navy, Chief of Planning Section K-16. Christenson's greeting was cool and perfunctory. "So you're going to help us plan this invasion," he mused. "You have any invasion planning experience?"

Stu admitted that he had none.

"Well," Christenson continued, "I'm sure you tried to do your bit. Tough about the crash-landing and getting grounded. But we are planning the beach preparation activities from H-Hour minus 48 right up to 30 minutes before the first landing craft hit the beach. Operation

Neptune. It's primarily a Navy show; not sure how a fighter jock can contribute. I know how you got here so I have to fit you in. C'mon, I'll introduce you to Reg Childs, your teammate."

Pilot Officer Reg Childs stood as they entered Room 4 and, with a friendly smile, firmly shook Stu's hand. Christenson instructed Childs to "Show Lieutenant Rittersberg the ropes" and turning to Stu added, "Couple of things Mister Rittersberg: Childs here is your lead and everything we do here is Top Secret. Don't remove anything from this hut and no shop talk outside. Clear?"

Having been addressed as "mister" in Navy-speak, Stu replied in kind with a smile, "Aye aye sir!" Without returning the smile, Christenson turned and left.

"I'm Reg."

"Everybody calls me 'Beefstew.'" Stu explained the derivation from his middle name.

"Well, have you found a place to stay yet?" "Right," suggested Childs in response to Stu's "Not yet." The Black Swan in Teddington is for officers. You Yanks call it the "Dirty Duck." Walking distance; clean and comfortable. They try their best with what they can get at breakfast and dinner. But the bar is quite good. It's small but I know they have one room open."

"OK," Stu replied to this friendly bloke. After Christenson's frosty reception, Stu was already beginning to like Reg Childs.

After a few minutes of small talk about how they both came to SHAEF, they found much in common. Childs was a Welshman, read Queuing Theory at Aberstwyth University before joining the RAF, becoming a navigator. He flew 44 missions in Halifax and Wellington bombers until he suffered a depressed left eardrum while firing the top turret guns at a German fighter. The depression further caused enough tinnitus for him to fail the flight physical and so, as with Stu, Childs was grounded to a desk job.

Their Room 4 workspace was a large table, piled with thick planning documents and "After Action" reports. The two airmen sat facing each other across the table and its piles of hundreds of pages. Childs gestured toward a large wall map of the Normandy coast surrounded by 8x10 inch black and white photos of beaches, small coastal towns, fortified buildings, and coast artillery casemates. The map was labeled 'TOP SECRET" and Operation NEPTUNE.' "That's what we are doing here," Childs said.

"Our task is to research the coastal landing plans of recent invasions and the post-landing "After Action" reports, looking for whatever in the plans were not well thought out or simply didn't achieve the intended results. We will also make recommendations to be included in the NEPTUNE Plan's Annex Dog[91] – the landing preparations intended to suppress German defenses along the

---

[91] Childs referred to Annex D by using the old phonetic alphabet.

Normandy coast and enable our troops to move inland off the beaches.

I've just finished reviewing Operation JUBILEE, the invasion of Dieppe last year that came a cropper."[92] Reg picked up a stack of reports and showed it to Stu. "We put over 6000 infantry ashore last August and 60% were very quickly killed, wounded or captured. It's obvious that Jerry's[93] coastal defenses hadn't been knocked out beforehand and the beach became a slaughterhouse. I looked into what naval and air support were planned: First-off, we only supported the landings with six destroyers and their 4-inch guns because the First Sea Lord wouldn't risk a cruiser or battleship without air superiority. Next, most of the pre-landing aerial bombardment was curtailed so as not to kill French civilians. I've made a note of both of those." Reg pulled another paper out of the stack he was holding. "Not least, every one of the tanks we put ashore couldn't move up the steeply-sloped beach, which wasn't hard sand but loose gravel. An after-action summary by Major Allen Glenn of the Calgary Tank Regiment said that worse terrain for tanks couldn't have been picked. The stones collected in the tank tracks and broke them. Every one of the Canadian tanks was stopped and destroyed by Jerry's artillery."

Stu jotted a note to recommend that all of the candidate beaches for landing tanks needed to be studied for suitability.

---

[92] Brit-speak for "failed"
[93] Brit-speak for the Germans

Royal Navy Ensign John Howland, a SHAEF intelligence analyst knocked on the office door, interrupting the conversation. Howland brought a slim white folder with red borders to Reg Childs and had him sign a receipt for it. Childs then signed and dated the "Accountability Control Log" on Page One before reading the enclosed document. After reading it twice, he slid it across the table to Stu.

"I think you'll be interested in this," Childs guessed. "Don't forget to sign the control sheet."

Stu read the G-2 report, stamped "TOP SECRET EDICT," both his thumbs moving up and back on the page, his head slightly nodding. Looking up, Stu asked, "What does "EDICT" mean?

Childs replied, "It means the information is from a one of our trusted secret sources. Probably in France right near the coast. I doubt anyone here at "HQ" knows who it is. We had an earlier report from the EDICT source advising that Jerry has been burying mines on the beach mixed-in with the pointy obstacles intended to rip out the bottoms of landing craft. After that report came in, we laid-on a photo-recce mission that got some very detailed pictures of the beach all the way from Deauville to Quinéville, just east of the Cherbourg Peninsula. They're on the wall over there," pointed-out by Childs.

Actually, "EDICT" was the codename assigned to reports from Pierre Fermier, the trashman from *Vierville sur Mer*, close-by the beach. But neither Reg nor Stu would ever know that.

Childs continued. "You've arrived just at the right time. One of your two-stars[94] has just been posted here from Hawaii. He led the planning for some of the Pacific island invasions and has been sent to us to advise on what works and what doesn't and what results in avoidable casualties. He meets with General Bradley on Thursday and then we will have an open-ended working session with him. I'm really looking forward to picking the general's brain."

---

[94] Childs refers to US Army Major General Charles H. Corbett

CHAPTER 28

February 1944 - Stu Sees Aircraft

 Stu found himself aware that long stretches of quiet were a rare wartime commodity in southern England. His aviator's senses were prone to noticing the sound of aircraft engines and, since the distinctive throbbing of unsynchronized German bomber formations was often drowned-out by the much louder explosions of bombs, Stu – like everyone else – could not become complacent.

Sleep was disturbed many nights by air raid sirens and the hurried scramble down to the shelter. Explosions close-by and far-off mixed with Fire Brigade bells and police whistles emphasized the grim reality of unpredictable danger. The roar of RAF Bomber Command aircraft forming-up to head for targets across the Channel filled what could have been the quiet hours but, Stu could tell from the note of the engines that they were British and, often, what types they were. In the cellar bomb shelter with his workmate, Reg, they often told each other what kind of aircraft they were listening to.

The daylight hours didn't offer any long quiet periods either. Large formations of US bombers and fighters were often directly overhead, loud enough to make conversation almost impossible. Adding to Stu's disquiet was his compulsion to look aloft wistfully, wanting to be part of an operational squadron with an important combat mission to accomplish.

On February 18th, General Eisenhower pinned both a Distinguished Flying Cross and a Purple Heart on Stu in recognition of his two Bf109 kills and his injuries suffered in his crash-landing. After pinning on the medals, Ike shook Stu's hand for an extended period, reminding Stu that he had known him since he was a baby and was "mighty pleased" at how he turned out. Stu's father was in the small group attending the ceremony as well as two of his former flying-mates from the 31st Fighter Group, who clapped him on the back and congratulated "Beefstew." But more than ever, Stu wished he was back in a cockpit.

CHAPTER 29

February 1944 - Stu's Epiphany

Tossing and turning, Stu couldn't get to sleep. He wasn't bothered by the soft rumble of distant anti-aircraft guns but his mind kept turning over the problem of how to avoid the deaths of so many infantrymen on such heavily-defended beaches. At about 2am, he rolled onto his side, instructing himself that lying awake wasn't useful; he could pick up the analysis in the morning and that it was OK to sleep. He was snoring softly in a couple of minutes.

But just after 4am, Stu's eyes snapped open; "Eddie Rickenbacker!" he recalled. Back at the Academy, doing research for a term paper, Stu had read part of Rickenbacker's memoirs[95] "Of course! This is what I've been looking for! This is something we can use!"

First thing next morning walking with Reg Childs from the Black Swan Hotel to Camp Griffiss, Stu enthused, "I think I've got it; can't wait to get inside!" The two walked silently through the entry gate to Hut 54 and as soon as he had shut the door to Room 4, Stu went right to the wall map of Normandy and began.

---

[95] Stu would have read Rickenbacker's, *Fighting the Flying Circus*

"I see the beach landings in two basic steps. Step One is the naval bombardment that ends at a precise time as the landing craft approach the beaches. Step Two starts at exactly the time the naval bombardment stops. In Step Two, low-level aircraft must immediately begin attacking beach defenses to keep the Krauts[96] in their shelters and knock-off any in the open or already in machine gun nests and mortar pits," Stu explained, tracing the bluffs overlooking the beaches with his finger. I call this *Close Air Support*."

Stu continued, "We attack in trail[97] - many aircraft. I haven't figured out how many we'd need yet, but <u>many</u>. The most critical part will be having a Command and Control capability airborne – above the action – probably in a bomber with room for a team of controllers and liaison communicators with radios. I need to think this through."

Reg had listened patiently, already full of questions but unwilling to press Stu too early. Instead, he started making his own notes and the keywords of issues to be addressed and let Stu work with pencil and paper. After 20 minutes, Stu looked up, saw that Reg was waiting for more, and went on.

"We need aircraft with a forward-firing capability: fighters, Mosquitoes, B-25s, B-26s, Beaufighters, A-20s. Everybody in trail, in tight. Come in on the deck[98] from the Channel, turn west as soon as over the beach – coming

---

[96] "Germans" in WW2 GI slang

[97] "In trail" means "single file, one behind the other" in aviator-speak.

[98] Aviator-speak for very low altitude; "treetop" level

out of the sun, everybody around 130 knots.[99] Strafe machine gun nests, mortar pits, anyone out in the open. Right turn over Cotentin[100] and back over the Channel, return to bases to rearm and repeat the attack."

"We would need fighters high above to deal with any Kraut fighters that show up," Stu added, thinking as he spoke.

Reg's lips were pressed tightly together; he nodded once. Stu continued: "I'd put a B-24 at about 5000 feet, orbiting over the fleet offshore. Should be able to stay up for hours. B-24 will need some modifications: radios, antennas, and radio operator positions for airborne controllers. All controllers will be on their own assigned freqs:[101]

- A lead Close Air Controller on one freq monitored by all striking aircraft to receive control info, updated targets, and the like.
- One freq for communicating directly with Operation NEPTUNE Battle Staff afloat. This one must assure that the naval bombardment by all ships completely stops at a prearranged time.
- One freq for receiving from Assistant Division Commanders ashore on Omaha, Utah, Gold, Sword, and Juno to request target prioritization and adjustment. Aboard the B-24, requests from the beaches would be passed to the Close Air boss, who transmits to the stream of attacking aircraft. Need to work out a shorthand for precise target locations and

---

[99] About 150 statute miles per hour

[100] The Cotentin Peninsula, also called the "Cherbourg Peninsula"

[101] Radio frequencies

target types. Guys in the cockpits won't have time to be looking at maps.

Reg stood and joined Stu at the map. "Did you think this all up yourself? Where'd you get this from?"

Stu recounted his recollection of Eddie Rickenbacker's World War I impromptu use of airborne command and control from high above his squadron's attack formations. "It was needed in 1918, made sense then and makes sense now. What do you think?"

Reg began a continuous nodding motion. "We definitely need to do better in the critical minutes after the offshore bombardment is lifted. I think I understand the Navy's reservations about hitting friendlies on the beach. After all, those ships may be rolling and the elevation of their guns may be constantly rising and falling. Just a couple of degrees could make a battleship's or cruiser's main batteries hit hundreds of yards short."

The two young officers spent the next three days calculating details about numbers of aircraft, where they should be based, how long the stream of attackers might be needed, how many times might attacking aircraft need to rearm and return. They kept running into knotty problems and unknowns that made it difficult to work out how to fit squadrons coming from different bases into an exaggerated snake-like formation and to bring the snake's head over the Normandy beaches at a precise time that would be determined – not by any event that could be narrowly scheduled – but by the best-effort landfall of the Higgins Boats,[102] subject to so many uncontrollable variables.

They also had to keep reminding themselves about security. The most senior officers planning Operation OVERLORD were obsessed about not tipping off the Germans about the invasion date or that it *was* Normandy. Any rehearsal of the low-level attack plan would be impossible to organize, coordinate and run, if for no other reason than it would be impossible to conceal, from observers on the ground, so many aircraft flying single file at low altitude.

---

[102] Landing craft

CHAPTER 30

February 1944 - General Cota's Tuesday Staff Meeting

An hour and a half into General Cota's Tuesday morning Program Status Meeting, Flight Lieutenant Will Temple, an RAF Photo-Intelligence Officer, showed pictures of several heavy concrete bunkers with narrow slits facing the beach. Some of the slits were open while others appeared to be closed by dark shutters. The bunker roofs were clearly massive in the black-and-white photos and extended well over the open slits. Some of the roofs had been covered in dirt. The briefer indicated one of the bunker slits with a wooden pointer and said, "Our intelligence assessment is that these are bunkers for machine guns and are designed for protection of the guns and gunners by a heavy reinforced concrete overhang. We have good intel on the concrete mix they used and the gauge of rebar steel used for reinforcement. We estimate that, ultimately, all will be covered with sand and dune grass for camouflage.

Temple tapped a photograph with the end of his pointer. "Over here at SWORD Beach,[103] Jerry has built reinforced blockhouses between beachfront vacation

---

[103] One of the Normandy beaches assigned to British and Canadian troops.

houses. We estimate that these civilian houses have been commandeered as troop billets and headquarters offices. They may also be used for observation and as firing positions for machine guns and small arms.

"Our ordnance analysts at Royal Engineers/Chatham estimate that the bunker overhangs would survive a direct hit with only superficial cosmetic damage by a 5-inch HE round or anything smaller. A direct hit on one of these roofs roof by an armor-piercing round from 10- to 16-inch gun coming down in plunging fire has a 70% probability of cracking the roof through to the interior ceiling but only a 20% probability of collapsing the structure. Of course, repeated hits in the same spot increase the odds."

"We have also looked at the bunkers' vulnerability to air-dropped 500-pound bombs and rockets fired from low-level aircraft. We deem all rockets currently available to be ineffective against these reinforced structures. After release, 500-pound High Explosive bombs will initially travel no faster than the delivering aircraft and – even if direct hits – will be many times less effective than large caliber naval guns firing much heavier projectiles traveling many times faster.

Flight Lieutenant Temple moved a couple of steps to another set of photos on the wall and tapped one with his pointer. "This rectangle is actually the roof of a personnel bunker. The walls and floor are below ground and, as you can see, the building is up against the land side of the dune." Making eye contact with successive meeting attendees, Temple continued,

158

"Gentlemen, what I'm about to tell you next is classified TOP SECRET EDICT – from a protected clandestine source. So no notes, discussion or references in any correspondence please. The roof and the below-ground walls are steel-reinforced concrete, six and a half feet thick. Nine cots and simple furniture have been observed carried into one of these, which has a stove for heat and has electric, telephone lines and water. Jerry is building many of these and obviously wants to keep us from knowing how many and exactly where they are. Our clandestine source has reported that a final step in their construction is covering the roof with sand and planting dune grass and bushes. To date, sixteen of these troop shelters have been positively identified. There may be more we haven't found yet and we expect that more will be spotted through continuing photo interpretation."

General Cota looked across the conference table at US Navy Captain DP Moon, "Please be sure to tell Admiral Kirk that I am highly concerned about these machinegun and troop bunkers and would like him to assign a high priority to them for the fleet's big guns."

"Yes sir, I will," Moon replied.

The next presenter was Major Leonard Poole, Royal Engineers. Poole reported that Professor Shotton[104] at the University of Birmingham had finished studying the geological structure of beach sand from the Orne River to the Cotentin Peninsula. Poole explained that the Birmingham study had two phases. First, beaches in Britain having sand with nearly identical characteristics

---

[104] Professor Frederick Shotton

were crisscrossed by tanks and heavily-loaded lorries.[105] In the second phase, explosions simulating the blasts of many 16-inch artillery and 500-pound air-dropped bombs cratered and rearranged the sand at varying depths to simulate the results of pre-landing naval and air bombardment. Professor Shotton concludes that both study phases indicate that the Normandy beaches will provide the required support for tanks and trucks.

After the meeting, Cota confided in General Omar Bradley, First Army Commander. "I still don't like the odds. I've read all the Intel reports on Omaha and stared at the photos of the obstacles and bunkers till they're burned in my brain. When I go ashore with the 29th, I don't want to get pinned down by all those machine guns waiting for us." With a troubled expression, Bradley, suggested, "I'm having a drink with Frank Rittersberg tonight. Join us and we'll pick it apart – after we review the 1912 Army football season and what we should have done to beat Navy the last game of the year. All we needed was one touchdown. One touchdown! How on Earth could we have lost six-nothing?"

The day after Stu's father had drinks with Generals Bradley and Cota, he called Stu and invited him to have dinner. Frank noticed right away that Stu seemed glum and asked him how things were going in his job at K-16. "It's OK," Stu replied unenthusiastically.

"Still miss flying?" Frank asked.

---

[105] Brit-speak for "trucks"

"I always will," Stu replied. "But I've come to grips with reality and I know I need to move on. I just wish I could make a significant contribution."

"And you think you can't where you are?"

"I've spent weeks analyzing the relationship between beach landing casualties and pre-invasion air and naval bombardments. I was hoping to find a way to reduce the casualties but I think I'm swimming against the current."

Frank pressed his son for details and listened patiently to Stu's Close Air Support and Airborne Command and Control concept. Coming so soon after his discussion with Bradley and Cota, a light flashed in his mind. "Son," he encouraged, "Keep on doing what you think is right. I can't be seen to be pulling any strings for you but I may be able to plant some seeds."

Following his father's advice, Stu continued analyzing the problem, trading ideas back-and-forth with Reg. It was Reg, the Queuing Theory graduate, who went to the chalkboard and roughly diagrammed the Normandy coast and an arrow pointing west along the coast's length. He labeled the arrow "50 miles."

"If the landing beaches are about 50 nautical miles long,[106] end-to-end, and we want to keep Jerry indoors for 30 minutes, we would need a stream of 100 aircraft, a half-mile apart, flying at 200 knots.[107]

---

[106] 57 statute miles

[107] Nautical miles per hour

Stu immediately grasped Reg's simple, elegant solution. "Of course! The stream heads south from the English coast, turns west and strafes to a turning point at the edge of Utah,[108] then heads straight back to England."

The two airmen spent another two days asking each other "what if" and "how about" questions until they agreed they had the basics of a workable solution to recommend. Stu called his father. "Pop, I followed your advice and Reg and I think we have it about worked out! I believe we can save a lot of lives on D-Day!"

---

[108] Stu refers to Utah Beach, the westernmost landing beach on D-Day.

CHAPTER 31

February 1944 – Questions for George Christenson

U S Navy Captain Benjamin Cooley was Chief of "K Group," SHAEF's Office of Research and Analysis and George Christenson's boss. Headquarters scuttlebutt about the planned Normandy landings was pervasive. Captain Cooley called his planners together and quoted General Cota, whose dislike of "the odds" was one of the concerns high on the list. Cooley then asked for discussion.

Lieutenant Commander George Christianson, Stu and Reg's boss, wished the subject hadn't come up this morning. His plan was to appear cooperative and effective at the meeting to smooth the way for his requesting Captain Cooley's recommendation that he be transferred to a cruiser tasked for gunfire support during Operation NEPTUNE.

But Captain Cooley called on him and asked if his analysts had anything to recommend. Christianson replied that his section had the issue currently "in work" at a high priority and had only preliminary conclusions that seem to be leaning either to increasing the numbers of infantry to improve the ratio of troops landed to expected casualties or increasing the number of guns in the naval bombardment.

Cooley didn't like Christianson's alternatives. "More troops in the first wave isn't the answer. All the available landing craft are already committed. And we have no more naval guns to add. We already have 138 ships tasked to open fire at H-Hour and we've scraped the bottom of the barrel. We need something innovative and workable. Keep at it." Cooley called next on Canadian Major Robert deLaurier to report on Section K-3's study of "swimming" lanes for floating Dual-Drive Tanks, that would use boat propellers to reach the beach.

CHAPTER 32

February 1944 – The Whirlpool

Stu was at the wall map of the United Kingdom and Western Europe. He had cut a length of string equal to 100 miles on the map's scale, representing the long line of strike aircraft in Operation BOOKMARK and was experimenting with thumbtacks at curving, zig-zagging, and reversing the string. His objective was organizing 110 aircraft, flying in trail, to join up from many different bases, fit into their assigned positions, and be close enough to the Normandy beaches that minimum time would be required from their order to attack until they were over their targets. On his mind was the need to avoid mid-air collisions as the congregating pilots might need to contend with pre-dawn darkness and reduced visibility at the lower altitudes.

The UK was a country at war in the spring of 1944 with round-the-clock military air activity crisscrossing southern England and its coastal regions, watched intently by highly suspicious air defenses constantly on the watch for enemy raiders. Stu was struggling with finding an area not over the many Allied bomber and fighter bases and otherwise free of restricted airspace. After two hours of frustrating moves of his string and tacks, his best option seemed to be a "U" shaped path over southern Wales but he didn't like it. He asked Reg to take a look.

Reg Childs' immediate reaction was that the formation would be too far to the northwest. Reminding Stu of what Stu already knew very well was that the critical success factor would be bringing the Close Air Support aircraft over their targets almost immediately after the lifting of the naval bombardment and that the precise time of lifting could not be accurately predicted. That meant a jumping-off point as close to France as possible. About a half-minute of silence ensued while both young airmen looked at the map, sifting possibilities. Reg spoke first.

"I remember several times returning from bombing missions in the dark, most of our Halifax squadron pretty much together or strung out some, priority for landing was always given to ships with wounded aboard. So, even if ten, twelve, or fifteen of us had gotten back a few minutes before damaged aircraft with wounded, we would be held in a circular orbit near the field 'till the wounded could be brought in. We called it 'stacking.' Suppose we designate an orbit area and have all our strike aircraft fly there directly. We could assign each section from the different squadrons its own altitude, all orbiting around the same central point. When the 'go' signal is given, the stacked aircraft would empty the orbit like a whirlpool in a draining kitchen sink.

Stu's eyes lit up. "I like it! Let's see if we can find a place close enough to Normandy that the dash across the Channel would be quick but the orbiting planes would not get involved with the naval shelling.

"I can think of two problems," Reg cautioned. "First, Jerry's radar will pick up the stacked aircraft and know something is on. And then, there is no way we will be able to rehearse the stacking scheme. I doubt anyone has ever tried to stack 110 aircraft."

"Right. But with all the naval shelling going on, Jerry will know we are there anyway. He probably won't be able to do anything in the brief time between the shelling and arrival of our aircraft. As to stacking all those aircraft, let's hope our guys have good experience at joining up in the dark and keeping in formation. I think it can work."

Reg drew an oval on the map with his finger. "Just off the south coast – near the Isle of Wight. Oxford Circus is a name everybody could work with."

CHAPTER 33

February 1944 - John O'Rourke visits Ben Cooley

The two weren't well-acquainted so their discussion was formal and brief. Lieutenant Colonel John O'Rourke, on General Cota's staff, got right to the point and made certain that Captain Cooley understood that he had been sent personally by General Cota. The question about low-level air attack timed to begin at the end of the naval bombardment caught Captain Cooley cold. "We are working on a broad range of options," Cooley fudged. "If we have been looking at low-level air, it's probably very preliminary and hasn't reached my desk yet. Tell General Cota I'll have something for him tomorrow morning."

Right after O'Rourke left, Captain Cooley walked to Lieutenant Commander Christianson's office. Putting the best possible face on the answer to General Cota's question, Christenson acknowledged disingenuously, "I have two fliers working on that now but it's still very rough."

"Well, somehow, General Cota has taken a high-priority, personal interest in that angle. Tell your guys to put together a very brief overview of where they are headed. No more than ten minutes. They need to be ready to answer when they expect to be finished and if there is anything they need right now." I will try to get them on the General's schedule for tomorrow morning."

"Very well," answered Christianson, already thinking of including himself in this development.

Down the hall, Christianson ruefully addressed Reg and Stu, leaving no doubt who was in charge. "General Cota is looking for workable options that would improve our odds for success on the beaches and Captain Cooley and I need you to brief the close air idea to the general – probably tomorrow morning. We only have ten minutes so a very top-level picture only. General Cota knows the casualty statistics from previous landings so don't spend a lot of time there."

Turning to Reg, Christianson suggested, "We only need one presenter, Childs. Can you handle it?"

"Well, no, actually. Stu is the author of the close air and airborne control concept. He'd be much better prepared to handle questions of which there may be many. I can introduce him with a very brief definition of the problem"

"OK then, Mr. Rittersberg. I guess you're it. Will you be ready?"

"Aye aye, sir," Stu answered.

"Anything you need from me? Christianson offered, hands on hips.

"No thank you, sir."

CHAPTER 34

Stu Briefs General Cota

There were seven colonels and naval captains already in the general's office. Captain Cooley introduced both Stu and Reg to General Cota but without acknowledging Lieutenant Commander Christianson. The Captain announced that Flying Officer Childs would define the problem and then First Lieutenant Rittersberg would present a new concept of low-level Close Air Support controlled by a team of controllers on an airborne command post. Cota sat up straight in his chair. This was something new.

Reg very briefly summarized the recent history of invasions from the sea. "Our analysis shows that casualties have been highest where the naval bombardment's results were less effective than expected or where there was no naval bombardment either to achieve surprise or to avoid civilian casualties. Dieppe – North Africa – Sicily. In the Pacific, Guadalcanal – Attu – and, a couple of months ago, Tarawa. And in none of those costly invasions were enemy defenders so solidly dug-in and fortified as what we are facing in Normandy. Lieutenant Rittersberg has an innovative approach for supplementing the naval bombardment with close air support.

Stu went through the concept in eight minutes. General Cota, with an encouraged expression, looked at the seven senior officers standing in the back, "Questions? Comments?"

One of those standing in the back was Colonel Frank Hill, formerly Stu's CO in the 31st Fighter Group. Hill, now on the operations staff of 8th Air Force, spoke up. "This has lots of promise but it's complicated with hidden unknowns. I believe we could make it work but we don't have much time. A bunch of US and RAF squadrons would be suddenly diverted from already worked-out plans and I'm sure pulling a heavy bomber from somewhere will be like pulling teeth. But this is a better approach to dealing with the beach defenses as the landing craft reach the shore than anything I've seen so far. The idea is going to need flag-level[109] ownership. I will tell General Doolittle what I heard this morning and I'll recommend he tell our planning staff to get in touch with Captain Cooley, here, to see what the way forward is." And looking at Stu, "Good work, Lieutenant! Good to see you again, Beefstew!"

Colonel Hill continued, "By the way: some of you may be aware that we now have a new type of bomb 'specially for low-altitude drops. It's called 'Napalm' and I think it may be just the thing for the Germans' hardened bunkers at the beaches. I've been wondering if we had a tactical use for it; this may be just the job!"

---

[109] Flag-level: generals and admirals

Cota and Professor Harmon

General Cota called British Army Lieutenant Colonel William Harmon to his office. "Good afternoon, LEFFtenant Colonel Bill," teased Cota, placing emphasis on the British pronunciation of "lieutenant." Harmon was a graduate mathematician/statistician, who entered the Army from an Assistant Professorship at Oxford.

"Bill," Cota began with both hands behind his head and looking at nothing on the ceiling, "The whole staff is skittish about the expected high casualty rates in Normandy because of the hardened machine gun bunkers and the artillery casemates looking right up the beach. Some of us are really worried that a daylight assault could fail and doom the whole show. I know you lot[110] estimate how many troops will be hit by the machine guns given the number of guns, rounds per minute, and the density of our guys on the beach, assuming that a high percentage of the machine guns are still in operation after the naval softening-up.

"Here's what I need from you – right away: rework the expected casualty rates, if we eliminate 25% of the bunkers and 50% of the bunkers and 75%. In the rework, assume we can also take out the 88mm guns right over the beach. One last wrinkle: figure out the odds of our guys getting up and off the beach, if those percentages can be knocked out. Can do?"

---

[110] Cota refers to Harmon's team of probability analysts in "Brit-speak" that he has picked up.

"Yes, general," Harmon agreed. "We'll get right to it," giving Cota a snappy British salute. Cota returned the salute in kind.

Harmon's team worked through the night and the math professor was waiting for Cota, when the general came into his office at 7am. Cota noticed that Harmon was unshaven and surmised that he hadn't slept.

"Come in, come in," Cota invited, motioning him in with his cigar. "I didn't expect you so early. I'm all ears. Howbout some coffee?"

MG Norman D. Cota

The general sensed beforehand what the reworked numbers were going to show but he knew he needed more than guesswork. Harmon reported a corresponding proportional decrease in expected casualties to elimination of individual machine gun bunkers. Casualty reductions of 30%, 60% and 80% had Cota's attention. The mathematicians also anticipated that men fit to fight after landing would account for some of the guns' elimination themselves. Harmon handed General Cota a folder of his worksheets and Cota offered him a cigar. "Thanks no, sir. I'm for some breakfast and I may have a short kip.[111]"

---

[111] Kip = a nap, in Brit-speak

"Good show, professor," Cota shook Harmon's hand. "This is really important and I appreciate you lot coming through."

Cota called the administrative section at SHAEF Headquarters and told its chief, "I need immediate temporary promotions to Captain for First Lieutenant Rittersberg and to Flight Lieutenant for Flying Officer Childs in K-16. Can you handle that right away? Those youngsters will be up against some tough cookies in the next few days and I don't want them pushed around."

CHAPTER 35

Air Forces Challenges to BOOKMARK

U S Air Army Air Forces Brigadier General Ralph Stone asked Norman Cota to drop by his office. Cota walked across the Bushy Park compound to "Widewing," a cluster of temporary buildings housing the Air Forces offices. Stone said that Air Marshal[112] Sir Trafford Leigh-Mallory, Commander-in-Chief of the Allied Expeditionary Air Force at SHAEF Headquarters, tasked him with reviewing the BOOKMARK Operations Plan.

"Without even discussing it with him, I can tell you what the Air Marshall's reaction will be," Stone began. "Sir Trafford has steadfastly resisted pulling his air assets out of a carefully worked-out offensive program aimed at German industry, strategic transportation, and fuel stores. He has already agreed to using medium and heavy bombers against the beach defenses on the night before D-Day and fighter-bombers against German Army military traffic heading toward the coast."

---

[112] Equivalent to US four-star general.

"The BOOKMARK plan diverts 110 aircraft at the most critical time from the "Rodeo"[113] strikes he has already OKd. Good God man, 110! Sir Trafford is bound to ask me why anyone should doubt the effectiveness of the medium and heavy bomber raids against the same targets BOOKMARK lays on for fighter-bombers only firing guns and cannon."

An annoyed Cota replied, "I've read the bombing plan and, frankly, it worries me. The mediums and heavies will be bombing at night from between 17 and 23 thousand feet. The Channel is all cold water and there is a high probability of low-lying mist that will at least partially obscure the small targets that need to be pin-pointed. I'm also well aware of the Circular Error Probable[114] for a single bomber aircraft – even with your new "whiz bang"[115] bombsight. And I don't fall for the "bomb-in-a-pickle-barrel" propaganda the bombardiers spread around. The reason large bomber formations all drop hundreds of bombs at the same time against a single target is because it is hoped maybe some of the bombs will hit it. How often does a whole Bomb Squadron drop on a single factory or rail yard and have to go back the next day and do it all over?"

"The Air Marshall obviously has more confidence in our bomber crews than you do and won't appreciate your attitude."

---

[113] Leigh-Mallory introduced wing-sized fighter sweeps into France, known as "rodeos"

[114] The military metric for estimating the probability of hitting a target.

[115] A reference to the advanced Norden bombsight, which calculated a bomb's impact point based on current flight conditions of the bombing aircraft.

A red-faced Cota stood and took the unlit cigar out of his mouth, pointing the wet chewed end at Ralph Stone's nose. "Goddamit, I still don't like the odds. I'm going into Omaha in the Second Wave with the 29th Infantry Division. Would you and the Air Marshall like to go in with me?"

Later, pacing back and forth before the wall map in his office, Cota decided that, if BOOKMARK was going to be implemented, he would have to go around Leigh-Mallory – to Ike himself via Omar Bradley.

CHAPTER 36

Cota and Bradley

After he had washed his face in the Officers' Latrine, Cota walked past all the desks outside Omar Bradley's office and went right in unannounced. He briefly saluted his former West Point football team-mate, who was now the Commander of the US First Army, tasked with the landings on Omaha and Utah Beaches.

"Brad, we have a serious problem."

Bradley, fully aware of Cota's continuing reservations about a daylight landing, really didn't want to be interrupted just then by a repeat of Cota's protests and spoke first. "Norm, we've already settled the daylight . . ."

But Cota cut him off mid-sentence. "No, I've bought in to a daylight assault; it isn't that. But I'm real nervous about the odds, if we give the Krauts anything like 15 to 20 minutes after the naval bombardment ends. If any troops in bunkers aren't knocked-off by the Air Force and Navy, just a few MG-42's ready for our guys will cause an awful lot of casualties."

Cota repeated, calmly, the logic he expressed to Colonel Ralph Stone about the realistic expectations for the dawn bomber strikes and then went through the analysis prepared by Lieutenant Colonel (Professor) William Harmon's team. I'm convinced that our odds of success and holding down the casualty count will be much improved, if we go with Operation BOOKMARK."

Cota went through the details of BOOKMARK for Bradley, who listened attentively with pursed lips. I think Leigh-Mallory will veto BOOKMARK in favor of sticking to interdiction plans inland against troops and tanks moving towards the beaches. All we need is a couple of hours to concentrate on the beach defenses and then Leigh-Mallory can have all his planes back. If all goes well, we'll be up off the beaches and past the Kraut defenses by then."

"How many planes in BOOKMARK?"

"110 fighters plus one bomber."

Bradley inhaled through his teeth, making a hissing sound. "I can see why Leigh-Mallory would oppose that diversion."

"I believe a hell-of-a-lotta guys are going to die needlessly unless we keep Jerry in his bunkers while the landing craft are reaching the beaches. I'm absolutely convinced we need to do BOOKMARK."

"What do you want me to do, Dutch?"

"Get Ike to persuade Leigh-Mallory."

BRADLEY, LEIGH-MALLORY, MONTGOMERY, AND IKE

Separately, General Bradley had taken Norm Cota's case to General Eisenhower. Ike listened carefully as Bradley faithfully presented Cota's position and underlying justification. Impressed by Cota's performance with him in North Africa, Ike was predisposed to consider his recommendations carefully. Ike agreed and said he would call a meeting of Leigh-Mallory, Bradley and himself. "I'll ask Monty[116] to come as well. Let's see what he thinks. By the way, do I understand correctly that BOOKMARK is the brainchild of Frank Rittersberg's boy, the one they call 'Beefstew?'"

Air Chief Marshal Sir Trafford Leigh-Mallory

The four had a contentious meeting. Leigh-Malory started from a dug-in position, desirous of sticking to already hammered-out plans of detailed complexity. He was contemptuous of an untested air warfare concept only recently "dreamt up" and not studied by recognized expert authorities. He wanted to have RAF Headquarters give it "a scrub." The Air Chief Marshall was still smarting from Eisenhower's recent rejection of his sincere doubts over the proposed night-time airborne parachute drops. Initially, Monty said little but his expression and body language seemed to support Leigh-Mallory's position.

When Leigh-Mallory paused, Omar Bradley jumped in and recited from Cota's script. In a short spoken paragraph, Bradley detailed the robustness of the small, concealed beachfront targets and their likelihood of surviving the naval bombardment He added an expectation of low-

---

[116] Field Marshall Bernard L. Montgomery

lying mist complicating the well-known difficulty of hitting small targets from high altitude.

Montgomery spoke up. "To me the case is simple; if low-level strafing attacks can improve the chances of infantry getting off the beach with substantially lowered casualties, I say we do it." He turned to the red-faced Air Marshall.

"Leigh-Mallory, we certainly need your air forces striking Jerry's reinforcements on their way to the landing beaches. Maybe we can move more infantry and tanks up off the beach faster and stop them together."

Leigh-Mallory recognized he was out-voted and didn't argue further and was silent for the rest of the meeting.

Ike looked at the other three. "Gentlemen, I believe this Close Air Support idea may help us with a problem many of us are worried about."

General Omar Bradley

General Dwight D. Eisenhower and Field Marshal Sir Bernard L. Montgomery

Close Air Support and the Airborne Control Post were born. Ike signed the Operation BOOKMARK plan three days later. Two days after that, nighttime Air Raid sirens sent everyone scrambling into bomb shelters. Ike and Frank Rittersberg wound up in a shelter together.

"Frank, I've seen some of your son's work. Very impressive. How's he doing after his wreck?

Frank told Ike that he was "doing fine."

Do you remember when I said you had to go get him from France back in 1920? Sure glad you did. Glad I had a tiny bit to do with that!"

CHAPTER 37

February 1944 - Navy Conditions ands Demands

"Let's all get something straight – right from the start," commanded a serious-faced Rear Admiral Eugene Bailey, Deputy Chief of Naval Planning for Operation Overlord. "I'm OK with the idea of Close Air Support starting when the naval barrage is lifted and an Airborne Command Post sounds like a good idea but there are several sticking points the Navy – and I include the Royal Navy and Canadians in this – want the final say on. Here's our list:

1. "The Naval Staff will retain control of any 'Cease Fire' order to the fleet. Starting at H-Hour, the Channel off Normandy is going to be one hell of a noisy 2500 square miles of salt water. We anticipate at least some German Coast Artillery fire that we will have to deal with and maybe some *Luftwaffe* [117] getting through. In all that excitement, there simply isn't an 'off' switch to throw. We have serious concerns about Communications Security and can't open ourselves up to the Krauts intruding into our Command Net and sending everybody a phoney 'Cease Fire.' In high threat environments, the Navy uses flags and

---

[117] German Air Force

187

signal lamps; we can tell who we're looking at. A radio signal could come from anywhere."

2. "If we go through with BOOKMARK, we want a Navy man on that Airborne Command Post and that's easier said than done. We ain't suiting-up a sailor and sticking him on a bomber with a radio and control of the largest armada in human history. He will have to be a senior naval airman with long experience in air-to-ground radio communications. We think we can detail a Mustang[118] with years of enlisted time as a Leading Petty Officer **of** Communications. He's now a Lieutenant flying Maritime Patrol PBYs[119] out of Iceland. Name's Palmer. If we can get him, he would be our guy. We've taken an early step of bringing him here to look over the plan and give us his thoughts. We will have him read-on for Top Secret access when he gets here."

RAF Conditions

Admiral Bailey had delivered his conditions in his best 'NOW HEAR THIS VOICE," which didn't invite interruptions and no one challenged him, except to ask how the fleet would lift the naval barrage. "Synchronized watches" was the terse answer. In response to a question about Lieutenant Palmer's arrival, Admiral Bailey said, "Thursday."

---

[118] Officer with prior enlisted service

[119] US Navy two-engine amphibious aircraft

Group Captain[120] Eric Watt raised his hand. "I am here representing the RAF 'Y' Service[121] and have come up from Chicksands in Bedfordshire. Afraid I can't discuss our mission – classified you know – but we have a lot of chaps, who are really good at protecting operational communications nets. I have reviewed the 'Security Section' of the BOOKMARK Plan's Section K and see it as incomplete. Tomorrow, Chicksands is sending Squadron Leader Gary Williamson to help with the review and suggest what more it might need.

Next, Lieutenant Colonel Carl Clair from 8th Air Force Headquarters reported that a B-24 from the 34th Bomb Group at RAF Mendelsham had been requisitioned and was now at RAF Greenham Common, ready for the installation of radios, radio-op positions, antennas and all the necessary wiring – as soon as we get a 'Green Light." Greenham says they received five BC-458A transmitters, five BC-348H receivers, and five LP-21 Loop fairings[122] to install on the bird's underside. You better believe the CO[123] of the 34th Bomb Group is having a fit and complaining to everybody he can reach. He also isn't buying that he's not cleared for the project."

---

[120] Equivalent to colonel

[121] That was the part of the RAF intercepting German Luftwaffe radio signals to produce Communications Intelligence (COMINT). No one in the room had a COMINT clearance.

[122] Antenna housing

[123] CO = Commanding Officer

CHAPTER 38

At The *Hôtel de la Plage*

Victor Couillard's aged parents owned the grand old *Hôtel de la Plage* in little *Vierville sur Mer*. The hotel, a six-story, 48-roomed white stone building was traditionally a popular summer vacation spot. Fully booked months in advance by *Parisien* regulars, the hotel was favored for its access to the beach and boardwalk. Its kitchen and wine cellar were likewise famous. The hotel was immediately commandeered after France's 1940 capitulation and used to quarter troops of Company 2 of the 726th Grenadier Regiment. It was Company 2 that manned the defenses overlooking what would come to be known as "Omaha Beach." *Leutnant* [124] Edmund Bauch, the Company Commander, allowed Couillard and his parents to live in one room of the hotel. He also allowed two cooks to live together in another room. All the other hotel staff were discharged except those in the kitchen: two cooks, two waitresses and a dishwasher.

Sophie Millot and Cécile Girard, both in their 40s and unmarried, had been the mainstays of the hotel's kitchen for years. Even with Chef Alex Dumont now gone, the two cooks were experienced enough to prepare meals to

---

[124] Lieutenant

the satisfaction of their German "guests." Fearful of being kicked-out with nowhere else to go, they gave *Feldwebel*[125] Lehmann, the Mess Sergeant, no trouble. They learned to prepare food according to German tastes: *schnitzels, bratwurst,* and *schweinehaxen.* Sophie even learned to like *goulaschzuppe.* Nonetheless, they despised Lehmann's coarseness, domineering attitude, and rancid body odor. Cécile also had a personal score to settle : a cousin had been found sheltering downed RAF airmen and was summarily shot. Routinely, Cécile spit in food she was about to serve her German masters, satisfied that she was striking a blow for France.

Sophie and Cécile were permitted – one at a time – to ride in the truck that made weekly resupply trips to the Army Group commissary in Valognes. Sophie was a supporter of the *Résistance* and, while Cécile confided that she was too, Sophie wasn't sure. Although they had lived as virtual sisters for years, Sophie didn't know if Cécile would take risks, when the time came.

On March 8th, Josephine Aguilon, from Barfleur, made eye contact with Sophie at the German commissary in Valognes and, using hand signals, communicated that there was a message in the gill of the fish at the bottom of the basket she had put in the back of Sophie's truck. Josephine had written the message herself in a "one-time pad" cipher that was virtually unbreakable. German soldiers watching civilians coming and going from the commissary didn't notice the secret communication.

Back in the hotel kitchen, Sophie retrieved the message wrapped in wax paper and concealed it in the hollow

---

[125] Sergeant

handle of a carving knife. Later that night, she decoded the message in her bedroom, using a text from the Book of Ezekiel in her bible as the key. The message was short and simple: "Brévard has a package for you."

After fixing and serving breakfast the next morning, Sophie rode her bicycle down the *Rue du Lavoir* to Phillipe Brévard's pharmacy. Brévard and his father and grandfather before him had been pharmacists in the same old house, which stood next to the church. She and Brévard chatted quietly as he put a box of feminine hygiene products on the counter. Sophie paid and left, riding back to the hotel with the unwrapped box in the basket of her bicycle, her heart pounding as perspiration glistened above her upper lip. No German paid any attention to her and she rode back into the hotel and started to calm down.

Later, in the bedroom, when Cécile wasn't there, Sophie opened the box from Brévard and discovered a container of *Marvis* face powder. As she had been previously instructed, she tucked the container away with her personal things. Sophie did not know that the *Marvis* container had been refilled with a very highly concentrated mixture of sodium phosphate and ipecac root prepared by Brévard the Chemist.

The formula for that powerful laxative-emetic had been developed in England at the Porton Down laboratories, illicitly transferred to a Soviet agent and secretly forwarded to Moscow. The Red Army's Military-

Chemical Administration (*VOKhIMU*) decided that it had a potential tactical use: contamination of a military unit's rations to achieve large-scale debilitation of enemy troops.

In response to Stalin's encouragement to support French communists in the *Résistance*, the *VOKhIMU* encoded the formula along with preparation and concealment directions and started the encoded message on its way from the USSR to Normandy. Later, Sophie was instructed to keep the *Marvis* container safely hidden until the date when she would mix it into food she would prepare for troops of the 726th Grenadier Regiment.

The message from Moscow had crossed the Black Sea by submarine, travelled across Eastern Europe hidden on trains, and was eventually smuggled through Germany to Normandy by communist anti-German railroad workers. Bernard Perrier received and decoded the message containing the powerful laxative-emetic formula and provided it to Josephine Aguillon, who had passed it to Brévard the chemist.

In early May, a Free-French agent with the code name "Marquette," and parachuted into France by the British Special Operations Executive (SOE), met with Perrier. Marquette asked Perrier to be ready for sabotage and other disruptive actions that would hinder German responses to an allied invasion in June or July. Four plan categories had been formalized for assignment to the *Résistance:*

- Plan *Vert* (Green) was railroad sabotage
- Plan *Bleu* (Blue) concerned destruction of electricity generation

- Plan *Tortue* ("Turtle Brown") covered operations intended to delay the movement of German reinforcements toward Normandy
- Plan *Violet* addressed cutting telephone cables

Perrier memorized the SOE's specific requests for railroad tracks, telephone lines, and power plants to be disrupted and fires to be set. Perrier kept no written notes. The SOE provided no specific dates and could not specify any geographic points for the landings. Perrier would be given a 48-hour alert window via the radio message, "*Simone a perdu un gant rouge*[126]" broadcast from England.

Marquette's tone was emphatic. "The *Résistance* is being counted upon for that critical support. Start getting ready now!"

---

[126] Simone has lost a red glove

CHAPTER 39

The Plan Comes Together: Operation BOOKMARK

RAF Air Commodore[127] Hugh Whitman called the meeting to order and checked to be sure that all the tasked air groups were represented in the conference room. There was a mix of Brits, Canadians, New Zealanders and Americans representing squadrons flying aircraft well-suited to heavy ground attack. Each of the squadrons had demonstrated proficiency in low-level operations.

"Right; you have all had time to read the revised "Operation BOOKMARK" Concept of Operations and individual squadron tasking. You should have noted that we made the changes agreed at our last meeting and I believe we have accomplished quite a bit since we started only a fortnight[128] ago. The main points:

- "We won't move aircraft to jumping-off bases close to the Channel. All tasked aircraft will launch from home bases. This avoids moving ground support –

---

[127] Equivalent to US Air Corps Brigadier General

[128] Two weeks

armorers, refuelers, maintenance, and the like plus all their kit.[129]

- Headquarters have baselined the OVERLORD[130] framework and timetable, subject of course, to further changes.

  - At midnight on D-Day, a major raid – well over 1000 aircraft - by Bomber Command and 8th Air Force will hit the full length of Jerry's Normandy beach defenses.

  - At 0545, the naval bombardment will commence with first salvoes directed to areas behind the beaches where Jerry's artillery is dug-in.

  - As soon as it gets light enough for fleet gunners to see their targets along the beachfront – we estimate about 0550 hours, the naval barrage will shift to those targets. Originally, that shelling was planned for 40 minutes but General Bradley just reduced it to 20 minutes. Landing craft for Omaha and Utah will start their runs timed for reaching those two beaches at 0630. So, at 0555, the Fleet Commander will issue a "Cease Firing" alert that the naval bombardment will be lifted in 15 minutes – at 0610. That alert will be copied on board the Airborne Command Post by the Fleet Coordinator. He will pass it to the Close Air Support Boss, who will immediately broadcast the Attack Order to the Close Air Support aircraft. Captain Rittersberg will give you further details in a few minutes.

---

[129] Kit: Brit-speak for tools and supplies
[130] OVERLORD: Codename for the Normandy Invasion

- It's 100 miles from the south coast of England to the invasion beaches so when our Time Over Target for the lead aircraft is given, we need to be standing by close enough to get there quickly and on time."

Whitman moved to a wall map with his pointer.

- "We have blocked-off an oval from the Channel coast between Portsmouth and Brighton to points 50 miles south. That oval is "Oxford Circus." Each attacking squadron has been assigned a spot on what we are calling the "Conga Line."[131] First to go in will be Mosquitos from Numbers 248 and 544 Squadrons so they will orbit within the reserved oval at the lowest altitude – 1000 feet. Each following squadron's aircraft will orbit 500 feet above the aircraft they are to follow to the target.
- "The attack order will be the codeword "ROADSIDE" sent from the Airborne Controller in the B-24, using callsign "Fast Eddie" on the frequency we will assign in the Field Order. What everybody will hear is:

   CONGA LINE - CONGA LINE - THIS IS FAST EDDIE.

   ROADSIDE REPEAT ROADSIDE

   AUTHENTICATION – XRAY XRAY XRAY (The actual mission authentication will be provided in the Field Order)."

- "Here's where it gets a bit complicated so everyone needs to get this part right. The BOOKMARK mission objective is simple: continuously strafe the enemy

---

[131] Refers to a fun party dance from the 1930s in which many dancers form a long line and move snake-like around the hall.

beach defenses from right after the naval barrage is lifted until our invasion troops are on the beach in numbers and moving forward toward the bluffs."

"The lead Mosquito will stay in their orbit until they reach Oxford Circus' Six o'clock position and will then turn to a Course of One-Eight-Zero, descending to 100 feet and increasing speed to 200 knots, heading straight for the beach at Checkpoint "Baker-Item."[132] The very end of the naval bombardment will be a salvo of blue and green smoke shells on the beach to mark the "Baker-Item" turn for the Mosquitos, midway between Vierville and the *Pointe du Hoc*. They then turn to the west right up the bluffs overlooking the beach."

Everybody else spirals down and departs OXFORD CIRCUS at the Five O'clock position, changing course to One-Seven-Five till they reach the mouth of the Orne River, here at Ouistreham. They begin strafing runs along the bluffs starting here at "SWORD" beach, following the curve of the coast and hitting assigned targets all the way to Quinéville. That keeps the Mosquitos at the head of the line so Jerry to the west won't have a few extra minutes to figure out that the strike is headed his way. When the attack begins, it will be dicey with so many kites[133] descending like a whirlpool but so long as everyone knows the drill, it should be all right; everybody spiraling down till at 1000 feet and leaving the oval at the correct clock position, heading for France, descending to 100 feet and following the aircraft in front of him, a half-mile behind."

[132] Former phonetic reference for letters "B" and "I"
[133] Britspeak slang for "aircraft"

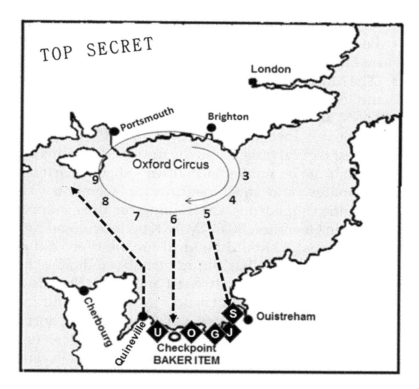

- "Each of your squadrons have primary targets and the latest recce[134] photos. Bunkers plus open machine gun nests and mortar pits are top of the list. Our Intelligence reports that Jerry has occupied private beachfront homes and small hotels along the Sword, Gold and Juno sectors to be used as firing positions. These structures are included in the target list for our cannon-firing aircraft. Ack-Ack[135] is still a concern, if any of their guns survive the naval bombardment, but if you are down at 100 feet coming out of the sun, they should have difficulty depressing their guns.

[134] Recce = reconnaissance in aviation-speak
[135] Anti-aircraft

Naturally, any Ack-Ack position is high priority on the target list. Also, any observed troop movements are fair game."

- "The Mosquitos – first in – will be firing their cannons and nose guns and dropping Napalm. The new AN-M76 100-gallon canisters. This will be our first use of this incendiary – jellied petrol[136] actually – against tactical targets and the first-in Mosquitos will concentrate on bunker structures – shelters, artillery casemates, and machinegun emplacements. The Mosquito squadrons are training for their Napalm drops in Operation BOOKMARK up in Scotland right now. Napalm should be ideal for the type of dug-in positions Jerry has put in just above the beaches all across the Normandy coast and, since there is no fragmentation, it won't send any shrapnel out into the water. The Mosquitos will drop slightly short of their targets causing the jellied liquid to splash onto the bunkers. One of napalm's drawbacks, however, is that it makes quite a lot of thick black smoke that may obscure the targets for the chaps further back in the Conga Line. But it will do the same to Jerry. There's no way to predict wind direction at this date so we don't know how long that smoke may stick around. There also may be some smoke remaining from the naval bombardment that will have just been lifted. Best we can plan for is that the leading Mosquitos will have had a clear view so we can use the line of napalm fires on the ground as a long target marker. Tell your pilots that if they can't pick out their assigned target, to empty their guns between the napalm fires and just a bit to the left – to the south."

---

[136] Gasoline in Britspeaké

- "Remember, what we need to accomplish is keeping Jerry from manning any of his machine gun and mortar positions along the bluffs after the naval bombardment stops and before our landing craft reach the beach. Our continuous strafing from the full length of the Conga Line should give our Infantry time to get ashore and start moving up before Jerry can come out to play. The last four Mosquitos will drop napalm on the big gun bunkers atop *Pointe du Hoc* but we have not assigned those as strafing targets. This could change if we get orders from Fast Eddie in the Airborne Command Post."

- "Oh yes. At last meeting there was a concern raised about flying at 100 feet over exploding targets. We have run it by Intelligence and they haven't spotted any ammunition or fuel stores along our strafing path so that shouldn't be a problem."

- "It is urgently important that everyone stays in the Conga Line until reaching the beach at Quinéville, the western end of the target area. The Navy will mark the Quinéville turning point with red and yellow smoke. The Line will steer north without overflying the Cotentin Peninsula - - too many Ack-Ack guns there - - climb to 1500 feet, remaining in trail while over the invasion fleet."

Commodore Whitman paused and took a step toward his listeners. With hands on hips, he continued, "Keep in mind: the shore bombardment will have stopped but everything afloat out there has anti-aircraft guns manned by jumpy sailors. They are expecting to see the longest string of aircraft in aviation history so tell your chaps to stay right behind the kite in front. No telling if Jerry might get any of his aircraft past our screen. Same for the Ground Observer Corps this side of the Channel. Once back over England, everybody goes back to home base for refueling and rearming to wait for orders to relaunch if needed, following the earlier procedure."

- "Lastly: we can't count on perfect synchronization of the landing craft reaching all five invasion beaches so it may be necessary to abort strafing targets at one or more of the beaches. That decision will be made on board the Airborne Command Post by observers with binoculars. If troops are ashore on a beach and already moving forward, the abort command will specify the aborted beach. What everybody will hear is:

> **CONGA LINE – CONGA LINE THIS IS FAST EDDIE**
>
> **ABORT JUNO – REPEAT - ABORT JUNO (or other beach)**
>
> **AUTHENTICATION – XRAY XRAY XRAY (Again, the actual mission authentication will be provided in the Field Order)."**

"And, if the entire strafing run must be abandoned, Fast Eddie will broadcast:

> **CONGA LINE – CONGA LINE THIS IS FAST EDDIE**
>
> **FROSTING ABORT - REPEAT - FROSTING ABORT**
>
> **AUTHENTICATION – XRAY XRAY XRAY (Once more, the mission authentication will be provided in the Field Order)."**

"In the event of an abort – one beach or the whole show – tell your chaps they must stay in the Conga Line right through to the turn at Quinéville. We don't want any friendly Navy Ack-Ack."

"Now, as to the Reserve Flight. The Plan provides for a section of ten Mosquitos to join the top of the spiral within Oxford Circus. Unlike the other 100 in the Conga Line, these ten will remain orbiting within the oval until they are directed by Fast Eddie to a specific beach target after a Strike Request from Beach Liaison. If the reserve is not needed, Fast Eddie will release them to go after targets of opportunity inland.

What everybody will hear is:

JELLYROLL - JELLYROLL - THIS IS FAST EDDIE.

BLOWTORCH – REPEAT – BLOWTORCH

AUTHENTICATION – XRAY XRAY XRAY (as before, he mission authentication will be provided in the Field Order)."

Air Commodore Whitman then called on Stu to brief the Airborne Control part of Operation BOOKMARK.

"The B-24 Airborne Command Post – Callsign "ICECUBE" – will launch from Greenham Common at H-Hour Minus two hours – 0345. We will orbit 50 miles southwest of the Isle of Wight at 5000 feet in the "Piccadilly Circus" oval during the naval bombardment. 15 minutes before the fleet gives its "Cease Fire" order to the ships, a 15-minute alert will be radioed to our on-board Fleet Liaison. The B-24 – Fast Eddie - will then broadcast the authenticated "ROADSIDE" attack order without delay. The Conga Line immediately begins the egress flow from Oxford Circus and the Airborne Command Post moves from Piccadilly Circus to a figure-eight orbit We'll come down to 2500 feet over the invasion fleet, five miles from the beaches from the western edge of SWORD to the eastern edge of Utah. The figure-eight keeps us closer to the beaches and we'll be watching the Conga Line hitting Jerry from east to west."

"The timing is critical – can't be overemphasized. The lead Conga Line aircraft, the first Mosquitos, will begin to overfly the fleet just as the shore bombardment is lifted. We are counting on the Navy to be sharp with their synchronized watches. I don't think we have anybody in the room, who wants to volunteer to fly at 100 feet through the biggest bombardment in history! [Murmurs of agreement and muted chuckles]. The Conga Line should reach the shoreline at Point BAKER-ITEM and at the mouth of the Orne ten minutes after the naval shells stop falling . We can't cut it any closer than that. Jerry doesn't know our timetable and is unlikely to start pouring out of his shelters in the first few minutes after the bombardment is lifted. By the time Jerry is ordered out and the protective shutters are opened in the bunkers, the Mosquitos will be lining up their strafing and napalm-dropping passes.

"Assuming the plan comes off without any glitches, Fast Eddie will release the reserve Mosquitos and will then recover at Greenham Common. However, if it is necessary to repeat the Conga Line sequence, launch orders for squadron aircraft including *rendez-vous* times in Oxford Circus will come from 8th Air Force HQ after a request from the liaison on the B-24. So everybody needs to get back to home base to refuel and rearm ASAP."

"Now, if the B-24 Airborne Command Post becomes unavailable for any reason, the authenticated "ROADSIDE" attack order will be broadcast from Fleet Central using callsign 'BARNDOOR.' Everything then goes according to plan except that abort orders and commitment of the reserve Mosquitos won't be possible. Questions?"

There were questions about whether individual pilots would be able to send information to the Close Air Support Boss and if they should expend all their ammunition during the strafing pass. A question about German fighters near the beach was answered by the Air Commodore. "During the low-level strafing runs, the 361st Fighter Group at Little Walden will put up 24 P-51s as a Combat Air Patrol above the Normandy beaches. They will be under operational control of the CAP Controller on the B-24 Airborne Command Post. Bandit sightings will be radioed to the CAP Controller, who will vector the P-51s. When the last of the B-26s in the Conga Line exits the beach area, the CAP Controller will release the 361st P-51s to seek targets of opportunity.

It had been a tense, attention-riveting meeting full of serious faces until RAF Flight Lieutenant Jocko Barnes gave everyone a welcome laugh with a question directed at Stu. "Ooos Fast Eddie then? That about your legendary reputation with the birds?"[137]

"Fast Eddie was the nickname of Eddie Rickenbacker, an American

Eddie Rickenbacker

---

[137] Birds = girls in male Brit-speak.

racing car driver and pilot in the last war. Captain Rickenbacker pioneered Airborne Command and Control and I'm recognizing him. Someday, I'm gonna tell him in person." Everybody looked expectedly at Jocko Barnes for his comeback, but he smiled broadly and gave a "thumbs-up" sign to Stu.

Air Commodore Whitman next introduced Squadron Leader Gary Williamson as a Communications Security expert from RAF Chicksands, joking, "But don't ask him anything about his job; awfully hush-hush you know."

Williamson described German capabilities for intercepting and understanding Allied air-ground radio communications and their capabilities for jamming or intruding false messages. He said that he had reviewed the allocation of primary and secondary frequency allocations and found them satisfactory with a couple of changes. He also made some "clarity" suggestions for the radio callsigns of the tasked Groups and Squadrons and uncovered a grid on a large chalk board, marked "TOP SECRET."

Conga Posit	Aircraft Type	Nr	Squadron	Base	Callsign	Freq
1-10	Mosquito	10	Nr 248 Sqn RAF	RAF Portreath	Keyhole	TBD
11-20	Mosquito	10	Nr 544 Sqn RAF	RAF Benson	Matchbox	"
21-32	P-47	12	62 Fighter Sq US	RAF King's Cliffe	Woodfire	"
33-44	P-47	12	313 Fighter Sq US	RAF Lymington	Porkpie	"
45-56	Beaufighter	12	Nr 404 Sqn RCAF	RAF Davidstow Moor	Postcard	'
57-68	Beaufighter	12	Nr 489 Sqn RNZAF	RAF Langham	Tiepin	"
69-80	P-38	12	402 Fighter Sq US	RAF Andover	Hardball	"

81-90	B-25	10	Nr 18 Sqn RAF	RAF Watton	Bowtie	"
91-100	B-26	10	596 Bomb Sq US	RAF Gosfield	Cowbell	"
Reserve	Mosquito	10	Nr 248 Sqn RAF	RAF Portreath	Jellyroll	"
B-24 Airborne Command Post			7 Bomb Sq US	RAF Mendelsham		"
	Cockpit Crew				Icecube	"
	CAS Boss				Fast Eddie	"
	Fleet Liaison				Skyking	'
	CAP Control				Hawksbill	'
	Beach Liaison				Chinstrap	'
	8th Air Force Liaison				Sodapop	

Williamson continued, "We have learned that Jerry has gotten good at intercepting and differentiating multiple tactical aircraft radios so that he can count how many may be heading his way. 178 B-24s bombed the Ploesti oil fields last August from Libya. Jerry heard radio operators tuning their radios before takeoff and was alerted to a major effort hours before they got there. We recommend checking and tuning radios the day before a scheduled op,[138] not everybody at the same time and keep it very brief."

"As best you can, observe radio silence. It will be tricky organizing the descending spiral in your Oxford Circus oval – especially since that's something you haven't been able to rehearse. Never forget: Jerry is listening! We recommend blinking your white tail lights as a prearranged signal to exit Oxford Circus and begin descending. Since each pilot is watching the aircraft he is to follow, if the lead gives – say three blinks – and everybody all the way back in the line repeats – everybody understands it as "Tally Ho!"

[138] Op = "Operation"

"Now about authentication. Air Commodore Whitman went through the Signal Plan to be followed by the Airborne Command Post and I'm sure you noted that the key strike and abort orders must be authenticated. Recently, Jerry has successfully intruded false messages into our radio nets, trying to confuse us, trying to get us to change course. He may also try to trick us into aborting the mission. Authentication for the key strike and abort orders will be a three-letter group spoken in the phonetic alphabet. To maximize security, we are withholding the authentication letters 'till the Field Order is distributed. Only one authenticator for the whole mission"

"Can I answer any questions about our Communications Security? There were none.

After various questions and discussions about radio procedure for reporting movements in the target area, filling a gap caused by an aborting aircraft, and who would be looking out for German fighters, the Air Commodore looked over at Stu.

"Captain Rittersberg, have we covered everything?"

"Yes sir. We have."

The meeting adjourned.

CHAPTER 40

Stu's Flight Physical

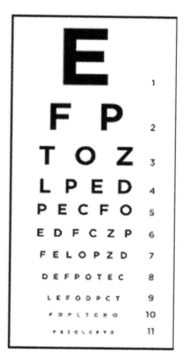

Army Air Forces regulations required Stu to be medically certified for serving as a crew member on a combat aircraft as opposed to flying as a passenger. In the clinic, a WAC Medic paged through Stu's medical file and then listened to his heart and lungs through a stethoscope. She took his temperature, checked his blood pressure, and had him say "Aaahhh" while depressing his tongue with a wooden spatula. Next, she asked about Stu's issue with floaters in his left eye. "No longer a problem," Stu fibbed.

"Cover your left eye. On the eye chart over there, what's the lowest line you can read with your right eye?"

On Line 8, Stu paused, then read aloud slowly, "D-E-F-P-O-T-E-C." He looked at Line 8 intently, creating a mnemonic for that line: "DEFEND PORTS OF THE EAST COAST."

"OK, now cover the right eye."

With his left eye, Stu couldn't see a single letter clearly on Lines 7 or 8 but he used his mnemonic and faked, "D-E-F-P-O-T-E-C."

"OK," said the Medic. "20/20 in both eyes. You're good to go."

With his signed-off AAF Form 20 in hand, Stu walked briskly out of the clinic without hesitation.

CHAPTER 41

12 May 1944 - The Greenham Common Visit

Stu and Reg Childs were flown in a UC-46 "Norseman" light aircraft from RAF Northholt, near London, to RAF Greenham Common, 60 miles to the west. The Norseman stopped close to the B-24 that was

UC-46 Norseman

being fitted-out as the Operation BOOKMARK Airborne Command Post. Tech Sergeant Len Corcoran, NCOIC for the modifications, was on the tarmac, waiting for the visitors. He introduced himself as "Corky" and took them on board.

"The two waist guns have been removed. All the 348 and 458 radios are installed in their racks. As you can see, all the seats and operator positions are in place. We attached the last of the Loop Fairings to the belly last night." Corcoran gestured toward two men in coveralls. "We are almost finished with the wiring. Tomorrow, we will start the bird's engines and test all radios – receivers and transmitters – and the intercom connecting all the installed positions as well as the bird's front end crew.

Stu sat at the table he had requested for himself, the Close Air Support Controller and put on the headsets that were on the table. By turning his chair, he was able to look out the open port waist window. Stu then stood and tried to move to the open starboard waist window but the headset cord was too short. He told Sergeant Corcoran that all the headset cords for each of the installed positions must be long enough to allow access to both waist windows.

Stu smiled and nodded his approval. "Looks good Corky. Call me and tell me how the tests went. The back-end crew will bunk in here two to three days before the mission. I will want to do a full Mission Readiness Test with all four engines turning and all the back-end crew on board right after I get here. Keep your installation team here and available, OK?"

They climbed out of the Liberator bomber and were looking at the recently-installed loop antenna fairings when Captain Earl Clark walked up and introduced himself. "I'm going to be your pilot. Guess we'll have a ringside seat for the greatest show ever!"

Stu wanted to know how much B-24 flying time Clark had. "Over 1800 hours in 9th Air Force. 25 missions – including that one to Ploesti that I'm not over yet."

"You see any problems with the mission profile – slow orbit over the Channel, off the Normandy coast?"

Clark shook his head. "Negative but you've taken away my waist guns, I'd be a lot happier with all my guns."

214

"That's a rog,"[139] Stu quipped while pointing to the Liberator's painted name, *Iowa Girl.*

"Wonder who she is."

"Obviously somebody in Iowa, who's missed. But this is still one of the 34th Bomb Group's ships and I promised Colonel Wackwitz to bring it back just as I found it."

"OK, "we'll take the Girl to the big dance but she can bring us home," Stu conceded, patting the B-24's nose.

---

[139] Short for "roger" or "OK" in aviator-speak

CHAPTER 42

May 24, 1944 / New Moon - Franceville: *Flakpanzers*

*O*berleutnant [140] Kurt Kaergel rode in the lead *Flak-Panzerwagen* [141] with another closely following. It was a very dark night with the moon in its "New" phase and the dawn still an hour away. Without headlights, the tracked vehicles inched cautiously forward toward their assigned position under trees close by the eastern bank of the Orne River where it met the Channel. Each tracked vehicle had twin 20mm *Flak-38* anti-aircraft guns and were there at the specific "suggestion" of *Feldmarschall* Rommel, following General Marcks' emphatic plea.

Their orders were to be in position from 0400 until 2100 hours[142] for the three-day period of the New Moon and the highest expected tides. It was boring, uneventful duty for Kaergel's men, who ordinarily would have been comfortable in town at Franceville. None of them understood why they had been picked for this duty that kept them from the bars and the music. They all thought it a punishment. Eating field rations with old, cold coffee didn't help.

---

[140] Equivalent to 1st Lieutenant

[141] A tank with an anti-aircraft gun instead of a cannon.

[142] 4am to 9pm

To kill time, Kaergel had the gun crew clean and lubricate all of the vehicles' and guns' moving parts but only during daylight. He looked the other way when some of the men found comfortable spots, curled up, and dozed-off. But until the sun was up, he strictly enforced the blackout: no cigarettes or matches, no flashlights, no interior lights showing through any openings in the vehicle. At the end of their long 17-hour days, the two mobile *Flak* units would return to their *kaserne* in Franceville.

After the third day, *Oberleutnant* Kaergel filed his report from the May 22nd to 24th deployment: "Nothing to report." He was hoping not to be assigned the upcoming Full Moon period – June 5th to 7th. 17 hours in the field made for a very long day!

CHAPTER 43

June 1944 - The BBC *en Français*

The Bedford Swan Hotel

Franck Bauer walked in drizzling rain from his rooming house on De Parys Avenue in Bedford to the Swan Hotel, next to the bridge over the Great Ouse River. "Another rainy day in England, he thought. He shook off his umbrella and left it and his raincoat in the vestibule before walking into the bar. Bauer always enjoyed the atmosphere of the old hotel, built in 1794 but even more, the bar and the blue-eyed, blond barmaid, Deidre.

For almost a year, Bauer had taken advantage of Deidre's friendliness in helping him practice his English. He had escaped from France in 1940 and was one of many escapees employed by the Free French, under General Charles De Gaulle in England. It often occurred to Bauer that his job didn't require him to know any English but he practiced often with Deidre, who always had an excuse for not going out with him.

Bauer was one of the French readers at the BBC studio in Bedford and Sundays were one of his assigned nights. For safety and to deny German bombers an opportunity to home in on London or Bristol using radio direction finders, the BBC relocated much of its broadcasting facilities to Bedford, 50 miles north of London. Every evening at 8 o'clock, Bauer or one of his counterparts, was at a BBC microphone, ready to read a set of prepared cryptic messages from a sheet of plain white paper. His instructions were to read each message twice with the same dispassionate tone. Bauer had no idea to whom messages were addressed, what their underlying meanings were, or if any of the messages were connected. He knew better than to ask any questions.

On the evening of June 4, 1944, Bauer was back at the BBC studio after having had a pint of Charles Wells light ale and a practice English session with Deidre at the Swan Hotel bar. At 7:30, he was handed three sheets of messages he was to start reading in a half-hour. He was surprised that there were 190 nonsense messages that evening, far more than usual. He prepared a glass of water in case his throat became dry and quickly read through every message to be sure all the words were clear to him.

At 8 o'clock, Bauer, wearing headsets, was at the microphone with his papers and glass of water watching Marcel Roche, the producer. In his headsets, he heard the first four notes of Beethoven's Fifth Symphony[143] and Marcel emphatically pointed at him. Bauer began reading immediately:

---

[143] The first four notes correspond to Morse Code "dit dit dit dah" for letter "V," a symbol for "Victory."

"Ici Londres. Les Français parlent aux Français. D'abord, quelques messages personnels[144]

Interspersed among the 190 messages, Bauer read:

- *Jean a de longue moustache.*[145] *Je répète, Jean a de longue moustache.*
- *Blessent mon coeur d'une languer monotone.*[146] *Je répète, Blessent mon coeur d'une languer monotone.*
- *Simone a perdu un gant rouge.*[147] *Je répète, Simone a perdu un gant rouge.*

And other messages, which translate as:
- Tomorrow, molasses will bring forth cognac.
- There is a fire at the travel agency.
- I love Siamese cats.
- It is hot in Suez.
- The chair is against the wall.
- The dice are on the carpet.
- Louis has two pigs.

1944: Chicksands Priory listening station

When he had finished reading the last of the 190 messages, he laid the papers on the table and looked directly at Marcel, who showed Bauer a clenched fist, signaling that the program had ended and that he was not to utter another word. No one in the Bedford studio knew where

---

[144] "This is London. The French speak to the French. First some personal messages."

[145] John has a long moustache.

[146] Wounds my heart with a monotonous languor.

[147] Simone has lost a red glove.

the next broadcast would be switched from or that Bauer's reading had been sent via telephone cable seven miles south to be transmitted by high frequency radio from the 240-foot tall antennas at the RAF Chicksands Communications Intelligence listening station. But Bauer and everyone else in the Bedford studio surmised privately from the long list of messages that "something must be up."

The great numbers of American and Canadian troops, tanks, trucks, and troopships in southern England were impossible to hide and the coming invasion of German-occupied Europe was universally expected. The 190 messages got the attention of the French *Résistance*, most especially those groups, which recognized a memorized message they had been waiting for. The long list of messages also put the German *Sicherheistdienst* [148] (SD) on alert, particularly the message *"Blessent mon coeur d'une languer monotone,"* which the SD had been told would signal the start of the invasion in 48 hours.

All over northern France, *Résistance* groups recognized their prearranged alert that invasion was imminent and that they were to implement various sabotage plans on the night of the 5th. Small groups of heroic French prepared to bring down telephone wires, blow-up train tracks or perform other tasks.

Wide-eyed Edouard Joubert, grabbed Bernard Perrier's arm, pulled him aside and whispered urgently in his ear, "It's come! *Simone a perdu un gant rouge.*" [149]

"You are sure?"

---

[148] Security Service, which intercepted non-German radio transmissions.

[149] Simone has lost a red glove.

"*Oui*! Absolutely."

"Go quickly; tell Josephine to come at once. Then 30 minutes later, you come back here."

Joubert only had to whisper the message and Josephine Aguillon was immediately energized. Her heart pounding in her chest as she tried to appear calm, she walked to Moreau's Bakery and went in. Perrier, who had been sitting at a café table across the street, saw her go in. He casually drained his espresso and rose to join her. With

Madame Moreau watching the entrance from behind the counter, Perrier and Josephine spoke for only a half-minute. She nodded her understanding and agreement very slightly. Perrier touched her arm as a calming gesture. "*Vive la France*," he mouthed silently.

Josephine went to Veronique's apartment and quietly told her sister-in-law the news. They agreed to take the truck to *Vierville sur Mer* first thing in the morning to tell Sophie Millot in the kitchen of the *Hôtel de la Plage* that it was time to act. At 6 :30am, they took six lobsters they had on ice and put them into a basket, put some ice on top and started out. Just out of Barfleur, at the intersection with the Montfarvile Road, Sophie noticed a pole stacked with German military road signs.

"I hate these damned *Bosche* signs. I can't wait to push them over and burn them myself."

"Do you think those dirty German pigs can really be driven out?"

"Only if a great many Americans come."

On the outskirts of *Lestre*, they were stopped at German checkpoint. Three bored, sleepy young soldiers, who had not yet been relieved after their midnight watch, came out to harass and ogle the women.

"So, where are you two pretty girls going so early? Let me see your papers."

"We are going to *Vierville* with lobsters for the *Oberst's*[150] dinner party at the hotel. We can't let them spoil in the heat of the day."

The third soldier raised the barrier and Josephine drove through, heading for *Sainte-Mère Eglise*. There were two more checkpoints going into and leaving the town. Their papers were inspected and the "lobster" story wasn't questioned. Ten minutes outside *Sainte-Mère Eglise*, they were flagged down by a German soldier, whose bicycle had a flat tire. They gave him a ride, with the bicycle in the back of the truck, next to the lobster basket.

The hitch-hiker's presence eased their way through the next checkpoints, where *Soldats*[151] Rademann and Manzenreiter opened the back of the truck and uncovered the basket of lobsters. "Why do we never get lobster? I don't even know what lobster tastes like."

---

[150] Colonel's
[151] Privates

Their bicyclist got out in Carentan, expressing a sincere, "*Danke, Vielen Dank.*"[152]

The truck finally rolled into the beachfront town of *Vierville sur Mer and* Josephine stopped in front of the Hôtel de la Plage. Josephine took the lobsters around to the kitchen door in back.

Sophie Millot and Cécile Girard were both at work in the kitchen and were surprised to see Josephine, guessing immediately that she wasn't there only to deliver lobsters. Sophie quietly sent Cécile to watch for anyone near the door to the hotel's dining room.

Josephine, close to bursting, whispered word of the "lost glove" message to Sophie, whose hand flew to her mouth. "*Mon dieu,*" Sophie gasped. "*Enfin!*"[153]

"You know what to do with what Brévard gave you. Tomorrow at dinner. Use it all and burn the container. Will you be all right?"

---

[152] Thank you. Many thanks.
[153] My God. Finally!

CHAPTER 44

Erdbeerenfest

Early morning, 5 June 1944

At breakfast, Sophie refilled *Leutnant* [154] Edmund Bauch's coffee cup. "I have been told that Germans like strawberries and have – how is it called? – *Erdbeerenfest* at this time of the year."

"*Ach, ja. Erdbeerenfest* [155] is a wonderful time in Germany, strawberries everywhere. I truly miss it."

"I know a farmer in nearby *Louvières*, who has some very large, very sweet strawberries that are ready to pick now. If you can give me fifty francs and let me have the truck and driver, I can get enough for our own *Erdbeerenfest* at dinner tonight."

"*Wunderbar!*[156]

Get enough for everybody in the Company. Tell *Feldwebel* Lehmann I said you can use the truck and that he should pay for the strawberries from the Unit Fund. I will invite

---

[154] Lieutenant

[155] Strawberry fest

[156] Wonderful!

Oberst Korfes.[157] We will all be very merry tonight, maybe even some singing!"

After Breakfast, 5 June 1944

Sophie told Cécile to bake enough shortcake for all their German diners plus a few extras for that evening and then left with *Soldat*[158] Klinger, driving her to *Louvières*. Cécile grumbled, wanting to know how she was going to handle lunch alone and bake the shortcake too. "Just do it!" Sophie hissed. "I will be back at lunch time to help you and we will do a simple dinner: wurst, boiled potatoes and sauerkraut."

Sophie was back at noon with 15 kilos[159] of strawberries and a can of heavy cream and began at once pinching-off the berry leaves, cutting each one lengthwise. When she had filled a large pot, she dumped in half-kilo[160] of sugar and some water and set the pot on the wood stove over low heat. Returning to the rest of the berries, she cleaned and halved the remainder and set them aside in a separate pot. Cécile continued to grumble about all her extra work. Sophie stirred the berry mixture and removed it from the heat.

The two waitresses brought the dirty dishes in from the dining room after lunch and left. "Be back here at five; don't be late," Cécile called after them. Cécile sat down for a rest, drying perspiration from her face with her apron.

---

[157] Commander of Grenadier-Regiment 726

[158] Private

[159] About 30 pounds

[160] About a pound

They could hear Noelle, the dishwasher, noisily racking dishes, around a corner, out of sight. As the hours passed, Sophie was feeling very anxious, commanding herself in her mind that she must perform her assignment.

 At 4 o'clock, Sophie went up to her room and came back down with the *Marvis* face powder container she had hidden away. It was in her apron pocket. The shortcakes were finished and ready to be filled with the berry mixture. She asked Cécile to fetch the can of heavy cream and, as soon as she was out of sight, emptied about half of the face powder container, containing the sodium phosphate and ipecac formula, into the berry mixture. Her hands were shaking uncontrollably. It was a fine white powder but completely dissolved when stirred with her long wooden spoon. She sniffed the mixture but could detect nothing different.

Cécile returned with the heavy cream. "We have to make whipped cream from all of this," Sophie said. "We can take turns. It will take us a half-hour but we can't be late with the dessert."

With hands still shaking, Sophie took down a big tin bowl and, when Cécile wasn't looking, emptied the *Marvis* face powder container and poured in the cream. She immediately began whisking the cream, looking carefully for any traces of the powder. She saw none.

"After spirited whisking for ten minutes, Sophie turned to Cécile. "Your turn. I must rest my arm."

They traded places. Sophie put a tray of wurst into the oven and checked the potatoes. Cécile took over with the whisk. Sophie said to her very softly, "Don't taste it and don't ask me any questions."

"Why? What have you done? You put something in the cream! Are you trying to get us shot?"

"The hour of our deliverance is almost here. We must each do what we can to help get rid of *ces sales bosches*.[161] You too! If I can't trust you to help me, I will cut your throat with that carving knife. Do you understand?"

Now Cécile's hands were shaking. Sophie touched her back. "Pull yourself together. We must be completely normal at dinner. Remember, I will be watching you so if you want to live to see a free France, you do what I tell you. You don't know anything. It's safer that way."

At 5pm, the two waitresses, Adelle and Denise, entered the kitchen from the back door and immediately began setting the dining room tables. "Beer glasses and sharp mustard," Sophie called out to them. "We are serving wurst and sauerkraut for dinner."

"Ugh! I hate the smell of sauerkraut." "Me too!"

At 5:30pm, the Grenadiers of Company 3 began noisily filling the hotel dining room. *Feldwebel*[162] Kellermann spotted *Leutnant*[163] Bauch escorting *Oberst*[164] Korfes and

---

[161] *Les boches: derogatory reference to the Germans in French. Ces sales boches: These dirty Germans.*

[162] Sergeant

[163] Lieutenant

[164] Colonel

barked, "*Achtung!*" Instantly, the room fell silent and the two waitresses knew they were also supposed to be still.

"*Bitte meinen herren,*[165]" said a smiling Korfes. "I am pleased to join you this evening. Thank you for inviting me."

Korfes and Bauch took their seats at the head table. All the Grenadiers sat and respectfully muted conversations resumed. Adelle and Denise brought out platters piled high with *rindswurst,*[166] and bowls of potatoes and sauerkraut. Next came trays with glasses of light beer. Conversations gave way to quiet as the troops began eating and drinking. When the troops had nearly finished their plates, *Leutnant* Bauch stood, beer glass in hand, and sang out loud, "*In München steht ein Hofbräuhaus: Eins, zwei, g'suffa!*"[167]

In short order, everybody was singing, *Oberst* Korfes as well. When the last stanza was finished, Bauch raised both hands for silence and announced that there was a special surprise for dessert.

"*Heute abend gibst Erdbeerenfest in Frankreich!*"[168] There was cheering and applause as Adelle and Denise brought out heaping bowls of red strawberries mounded-over with whipped cream. Sophie had warned the waitresses not to eat any of the dessert themselves because there might not be enough to go around. The girls were used to being told not to eat any of the Germans' food. Usually, they ignored it.

---

[165] Please gentlemen.

[166] Beef sausages

[167] The famous German drinking song, "In Munich there is a Hofbrauhouse: One, Two, chug-a-lug."

[168] This evening we have *Eerdbeerenfest in France.*

The Grenadiers piled the treat on their plates. *Soldat* Dieter Roeder was just about to dig into his when *Feldwebel* Kellermann, sitting across from him, pulled Dieter's plate away. "None for you *Ungeschickte Nudel Finger!*"[169] Dieter watched morosely as Kellermann lustily ate two servings of the strawberries and cream.

There was more singing after dessert until *Oberst* Korfes whispered in *Leutnant* Bauch's ear. "We are in the full moon period and must remain vigilant. Skeleton crews in bunkers tonight, everybody else on ready alert in quarters. Korfes and Bauch stood up. The Grenadiers snapped to attention. Korfes repeated his thanks for a wonderful evening and bid the men, "Good night."

Bauch reminded his men of the on-going alert and repeated Korfes instructions.

---

[169] "Worthless noodle-fingers

CHAPTER 45

June 5, 1944 / Full Moon - Franceville

To his disappointment, *Leutnant* Kaergel did draw the Orne River deployment assignment again but picked two other gun crews, who had all heard from the May deployment that it wasn't to be a fun trip. Much grumbling ensued and the 17-hour shift starting on June 5th was a repeat of numbing boredom. They were all grateful to head back to town at 9pm for beer and hot food and early to bed for their 3am wake-up and back out to the river again.

Shortly after midnight on June 6th, everyone in Franceville was awaken by air raid sirens and then thousands of exploding bombs dropped by 1200 Allied aircraft high overhead. The bombs were falling inland, well away from the beaches, and German troops and French civilians took to shelters fully aware that a massive air raid was in progress well to the south. When it was over, most got back to sleep.

Kaergel's two *Flak-38* units left town at 0340 and arrived at their assigned spot right at 0400. It seemed the start of repeated boring, wasted time. In the pre-dawn darkness, the *Oberleutnant* arranged for two-hour watches and he went to sleep in an uncomfortable chair. Only the lapping surf and wind in the trees broke the otherwise stillness.

Sleep was ended by the Allied naval bombardment, which started at 0555 with many heavy shells fired at German artillery and tank units several miles inland. Fully awake after only a few seconds, *Oberleutnant* Kaergel picked out the distinctive sound of artillery projectiles overhead.

Flak-Panzerwagen

He stood up in his *Flak-Panzerwagen* and, looking out to the northwest, saw clearly the distant flashes of the naval guns. He yelled, "Alarm!" to wake all his men and grabbed his binoculars. There were flashing guns as far to the west as he could see. "Start the engine," he shouted in a stressed high-pitched voice and when there was engine power generating electric for his VHF radio, he called the Watch Center in Franceville, which was already receiving similar reports.

"What are my orders," asked Kaergel.

"Standby and monitor this channel," he was told.

In the slowly greying sky, minutes before sunrise, Kaergel's jaw dropped as he beheld the size of the offshore fleet, whose gunners were by then able to see their targets along the beaches. They switched the massive barrage from inland targets to the coastal defense emplacements. In numb disbelief, Kaergel and all his gunners watched from ringside seats as the ships began shelling what would soon be SWORD Beach. No projectiles were exploding on his side of the Orne River and Kaergel expected to receive orders by radio but he wasn't being called. His deep-rooted German Army discipline controlled his thinking; his last order was to stay put and wait. He ordered all four 20mm guns loaded and all the ammunition possible brought up from the magazines.

At 0610, all the naval guns stopped firing but they could hear the crackling of flames and buildings collapsing in the little town of *Lion sur Mer*, a mile up the coast. Out in the Channel, Kaergel could see men climbing down nets into landing craft. *It was the invasion! Here, in Normandie!* He tried to inform the Watch Center by radio but could not get a reply.

CHAPTER 46

Just after Midnight, 6 June

Air Raid sirens wailed in small coastal towns and inland villages across Normandy as the sounds of large formations of bombers roared overhead. Troops in full battle dress sprinted the short distances from their billets to bunkers and shelters. Months had passed since Allied bombers based in England had been redirected to targets in Germany and no longer overflew Normandy. The troops were used to single high-speed, low-level photo-reconnaissance Spitfires screaming just above their heads and occasional attacks on anti-aircraft batteries a half-mile inland. Tonight was different. Tonight it was much louder, coming from a black sky with a bright moon.

Flakregiment 32's crews of 20mm and 37mm Ack-Ack guns that had been ordered to positions just south of the beaches, fired many thousands of rounds up at the bombers crossing overhead. Several batteries ran out of ammunition.

Unaware that it was specifically *they* who were targeted but missed by the 1200 bombers above, the Infantry and Coast Artillerymen near the beaches stayed undercover, listening to the explosions of many bombs well away from the coast.

Poor visibility hampered Allied bomb-aimers, who wanted to avoid dropping on the houses of French civilians and so, the pre-invasion air bombardment proved to be ineffective at neutralizing the German beach defenders.

After a short quiet interval, great numbers of other aircraft flew in from over the Channel heading south at altitudes lower than the earlier bomber formations. This huge flock passing in the dark sounded unusual. Searchlights criss-crossed the black sky and all the nearby anti-aircraft guns banged away but no bombs were dropped near the beaches. Alert watchers in the beach-front bunkers reported that there was nothing to report on the sand or in the surf. An hour later, it was quiet again, except for distant small-arms fire to the south. Most troops went back to bed. What had disturbed their sleep for the second time that night was the roar of hundreds of transport aircraft carrying paratroopers or towing gliders.

Sophie had confided in Cécile that they would need to be ready to get out of the hotel and move quickly away from the beach. Sophie wasn't sure what was about to happen but feared being questioned about the tainted strawberry dessert. At the sound of the Air Raid sirens, the two cooks, carrying only small items in their purses, went down to the kitchen, and then into the below-ground cellar. The whole hotel building rattled above them as they stood, trembling and unsure of what to do next. Cécile was a nervous wreck, paralyzed with terror, murmuring incoherently. When the sounds of bombers overhead had stopped, Sophie tried to get Cécile to move to the back door of the building and get out but she wouldn't, couldn't budge. Sophie tried to convince herself that she needed to abandon Cécile and make her own way but didn't trust her to keep the secret of the adulterated dessert. She continued trying to calm Cécile and convince her that they must leave.

The sky began turning grey in the east at 5am. It was at about that time that the first Grenadiers of Company 3 were awakened by cramps and a vague feeling of nausea. Within minutes, many were vomiting violently where they sat or lay, unable to stand. Those, who thought they could control their unwell feelings, were overwhelmed by the spectacle of many of their comrades throwing up with strangling sounds. Those able to stand and walk went to the bunker's latrine and quickly occupied all the toilets. They heard their comrades' anguished pleas to "hurry up and let me in" but none could comply. *Feldwebel* Kellermann, who had eaten his dessert as well as Dieter Roeder's, made for the exit door, retching and vomiting forcefully on the wall and door. Once outside, he sunk to the ground, simultaneously expelling vomit and diarrhea. Other Grenadiers followed Kellermann and joined him on the ground, completely disabled. Inside, Dieter Roeder vomited too – not because he had been sickened by the contaminated dessert – but because he was overcome by the horror he was witnessing. Dieter retreated to a corner and tried to shut out the awful sights and sounds. Separately, in their billets, *Oberst* Korfes in the *Château de Sully* and *Leutenant* Bauch in *Hôtel de la Plage*, were down the hall in their WCs, experiencing the same debilitating effects as their Grenadiers.

Naval bombardment of areas behind the beach commenced at 0545, while it was still dark, with the gunners waiting to switch to pre-assigned targets along the beach as soon as it was light enough to see, five minutes later. During the bombardment, thousands of Allied troops climbed down from troopships into landing craft that headed for their assigned beach locations.

It was light enough at 0550 and hundreds of large-caliber naval guns began firing salvoes of high-explosive projectiles at the defensive emplacements all along the Normandy beaches from "Sword" to "Utah." Hundreds of heavy projectiles fired by 138 ships exploded on and around Rommel's "Atlantic Wall" defensive emplacements. Thirty seconds before 6am, two 14-inch projectiles hit the beachfront façade of the *Hôtel de la Plage* in *Vierville* and a third hit on the street just outside. Those were among 73 others from 10 to 16 inches in diameter that came down in the little resort town that morning. Large chunks of the hotel flew in all directions and the remainder crashed down into the cellars, crushing Sophie Millot and Cécile Girard, who had never left the building. Victor Couillard, the hotel owner, and his aged parents also died instantly in the massive blast, joining over 3000 other French civilians killed during the Normandy invasion. *Leutenant* Bauch died sitting in the WC, his pajama bottoms around his ankles.

In his sumptuous *Château de Sully* quarters, miles inland, *Oberst* Korfes was unable to leave the oversized *salle de bain*[170] with its polished marble and gold accents, powerless to quell the forceful vomiting and diarrhea. He heard the bombing near the coast but didn't know what was going on. Suffering excruciating cramps and sweating profusely, Korfes berated himself, "I should have known better than to have eaten whipped cream on top of all that sauerkraut."

[170] Bathroom

Adelle and Denise, the *Hôtel de la Plage* waitresses, hadn't been able to resist scraping the bottoms of the dessert serving bowls and both were sick for hours in their parents' homes, several miles from the beach. Both girls heard a great many explosions near the beach but were unable to stray from the outhouses in their back yards.

When the Air Raid siren woke them just before midnight, troops of the 736th *Infanterie Regiment,* asleep in the commandeered *Hôtel Dauphine* in the town of *Lion sur Mer*, sprinted to their reinforced bunkers, just outside. The torrent of 500-pound High Explosive bombs, falling well south of the town from hundreds of Allied bombers, shook their bunkers but caused no damage. Four artillery casemates[171] on the bluffs at *Longues-sur-Mer* were priority targets for the bombers overhead but they missed, dropping instead on the town of *Longues-sur-Mer* itself and causing great damage. The "All Clear" sounded at 0120 hours and sleepy, confused troops went back to their beds in the hotel, which hadn't been hit.

HMS Rodney bombards Normandy

At 0545 hours in the *Hôtel Dauphine*, sleep was again interrupted, this time by a cacophony of mixed noises: the bangs of big naval guns just offshore, the rushing rattle of heavy projectiles passing overhead, and their explosive "crumps" inland. The alarm bells on each floor of the hotel added to the commotion as agitated soldiers ran for the bunkers for the second time. Ten

---

[171] Casemates: Fortified artillery bunkers

minutes later, multiples of heavy naval projectiles began exploding on the beach, along the sea wall, and against beachfront houses and hotels in the town of *Lion sur Mer*.

The *Hôtel Dauphine* and, across *Rue de Ouistreham*, the *Hôtel de Lys* had been identified by intelligence agents in Normandy as troop billets. On the flat roof of the all-brick *Hôtel Dauphine*, the 736th *Infanterie* had installed a 7.5cm artillery piece and two MG-42 machine gun tripods. Both hotels were designated as targets for the naval gunners as well as the concrete bunkers just behind the sea wall. Intelligence also identified beachfront vacation homes, now in German hands, as having machine guns at the windows. The first salvoes reduced the *Hôtel Dauphine* to a pile of bricks and blew gaping holes in the beachfront façade of the *Hôtel de Lys*. In just one minute, every window and mirror in *Lion sur Mer* was broken and many structures were on fire. A German concrete bunker sat only ten feet from a palatial beach home at 42 *Rue de Ouistreham*, which was burning. The mostly-wood building was soon fully ablaze, fanned by a steady wind blowing out of the northwest.

Infantrymen in the bunker were shaken by the enormous noise but were unscathed in their buttoned-up shelter. The wind, however, transformed the next-door fire into a blowtorch directed squarely against the concrete wall and dense smoke began seeping into the bunker's ventilation ports. Panicky troops, finding it very hot and hard to breathe, had to be restrained by their NCOs from opening doors to get out. Everyone dropped to the floor, desperate for breathable air.

The buzzer sounded on the field radio hanging on the wall. *Gefreiter* [172] Albrechts got up, grabbed the radio, and got back down on the floor. Coughing uncontrollably from the smoke, all he could do was listen. He suppressed the cough long enough to croak that the Artillery Observer in the church tower in *Colville*[173] was reporting hundreds of ships in the Channel and many landing craft approaching the beach. That alert was also received by all the other Infantry and Artillery units along the 50-mile stretch of Normandy beaches.

When the naval bombardment started in the *Vierville sur Mer* area at 0550, uncontrollable vomiting and diarrhea continued to disable the Grenadiers of Company 2, 726th Regiment. The doors and shutters were open and half the men were on the ground outside. All those outside were killed by artillery blasts where they lay. Those still inside were helplessly incapacitated. *Soldat* Dieter Roeder had stopped vomiting but was paralyzed by the din of hundreds of nearby big explosions, some hitting the roof of the bunker. Projectiles hitting the beach flung a hailstorm of sand and shrapnel against the bunker, some of it entering the machine gun windows at high velocity. Roeder's ears were ringing and he was coated in sooty sand.

Everything went strangely quiet at 0610 hours. The naval shelling had stopped. In all the beachfront bunkers, officers and NCOs listened warily for some confirmation that the shelling had stopped and could not be restarted because landing craft were near the beach. In one of the *Grandcamp.* bunkers, *Leutnant* Stahl ordered the doors and

---

[172] Corporal
[173] about a half-mile from the beach

shutters opened. "Let's get some air in here. Everybody get your things and stand-by to go to Battle Stations."

Machine gunners opened the armored window shutters and set up their MG-42s. One of them called out excitedly, "Landing craft approaching – one kilometer!"

At the *Vierville sur Mer* bunker, Klaus Hammer, Dieter Roeder's gun crew leader, was still in the throes of his uncontrollable double-evacuation. He knew he was supposed to lead his two men outside and set up the MG-42 machine gun. Hammer raised his head to look for his assistant, Rolf Emmerich, but couldn't see him in the tangle of bodies awash in vomit and excrement. He did spot Dieter Roeder, with a horrified expression on his face and was about to tell him to get ready when his stomach tightened and he retched, bringing up only bitter-tasting yellow fluid. Hammer gave up and sank back down. He tried unsuccessfully to get up a few minutes later. Dieter Roeder shook uncontrollably with fear; all parts of his body in motion except his feet.

CHAPTER 47

---

6 June 1944 – The D-Day Landings and Operation BOOKMARK

W hen the Higgins landing craft started their runs for the beaches, a cold, steady wind was blowing from the northwest, adding to the higher-then-expected swells that rolled the flat-bottomed boats uncomfortably. Having

Actual June 6, 1944 photo showing wind from the northwest blowing smoke inland
US Naval History & Heritage Command

eaten a *bon voyage* send-off breakfast of greasy bacon, scrambled eggs and buttered toast served by their well-intentioned Navy hosts, many of the troops were seasick and vomiting.

The naval bombardment was in full play, firing over the heads of the troops in the landing craft, their thunderous booms – louder than anything they had ever heard - making them cringe and their ears ring.

A thin stripe of grey on the eastern horizon signaled the oncoming dawn. Dilly Combes, Commanding Officer of Number 248 Fighter Squadron looked up and around the night sky and saw the navigation lights of stacked Close Air Support aircraft all orbiting within the "Oxford Circus" oval. RAFVR[174] Flying Officer Arthur Wythe, sitting next to Combes in their twin-engine wooden Mosquito, checked his watch and showed it to Combes.

It was 0549 and they were heading southwest; 109 other aircraft in the Conga Line were following behind and above. At 0550, numerous bright flashes of light briefly illuminated ships below and to the south that were otherwise invisible from 1000 feet up in the dark. The fleet had begun the pre-invasion naval bombardment. Combes and Wythe lost their view of the fleet as their constant clock-wise turn put them on a northerly heading.

On board the B-24, droning slowly off the Isle of Wight, US Navy Lieutenant Tim Palmer studied his watch and announced to his fellow controllers that the naval barrage would be lifted in fifteen minutes. Immediately, Stu pressed the "push-to-talk" button and spoke into his microphone and the Airborne Command Post came on the air just a few seconds after 0555:

"CONGA LINE - CONGA LINE - THIS IS FAST EDDIE.

ROADSIDE REPEAT ROADSIDE

AUTHENTICATION CHARLIE PETER HOW – REPEAT - CHARLIE PETER HOW"

"That's it, let's go," Combes said, pushing the throttles forward to increase the RPMs of the Mosquito's two Rolls-Royce Merlin engines while easing the yoke forward to

---

[174] Royal Air Force Volunteer Reserve

lose altitude. Artie Wythe toggled the white navigation light in the tail and both officers saw momentary blinking above and off the starboard wing as the rest of the formation repeated the blinking-light signal.

Anxious to get over the invasion beaches, Combes felt a twinge of impatience; the "GO" command came in while they were at the 10 o'clock position of Oxford Circus and Combes had to resist the impulse to cut straight across to their 6 o'clock egress point. But it felt better to have sped up to 200 knots.

 As they led their Mosquito section out of Oxford Circus heading due south, Artie Wythe expressed the hope that the ships would stop firing on time. Down at 100 feet and roaring over the now-silent fleet, crews in all the Conga Line aircraft looked left and right in awe at the greatest armada they had ever seen. As they sped past, landing craft could be seen up against troopships as infantry troops climbed down rope nets.

The sun was just breaking the horizon as the lead Mosquito neared the coast. Fires and smoke from the naval bombardment became visible on and behind the bluffs. A stiff breeze was blowing the smoke away from the beach and their targets, benefitting the pilots. And there, on the sand, were drifting clouds of blue and green smoke, courtesy of the Fleet, marking Point BAKER-ITEM and their planned turn to the west.

With the morning sun behind them, features on the ground were easily recognizable. Artie Wythe had a map and cut-out sections of photos on his lap and was tracing the map with his finger. "There's our first bunker just coming up." Combes eased the Mosquito to the left pointing its nose at the bunker, maintaining airspeed and altitude. Just before overflying the bunker, Wythe pulled the release and their two Napalm canisters tumbled awkwardly, hitting the ground and rupturing twenty yards away, splashing the concrete building with a wave of burning gasoline. They couldn't see the result now behind them but in Mosquito Number Two, a half-mile back, both crewmembers were shocked by the spectacle, never having seen napalm used against actual targets. "Poor devils. I wouldn't want to be in there."

At 0622, Mosquito pilot Dilly Combe's 20mm cannon shells hit on and around Company 2's bunker and his Mosquito roared overhead as Dieter Roeder cowered inside, his hands over his ears. In four minutes, machine gun bullets from Mosquito Number 2 banged against the concrete walls and roof. Almost four more minutes later, Mosquito Number 3 dropped two Napalm canisters that coated Company 2's bunker in gasoline burning at over 2000 degrees Fahrenheit. The conflagration quickly consumed all the oxygen in the bunker and dragon claws of flame invaded the open doorways and gun windows. The heat was merciless and hypoxia began to affect everyone inside. As the searing flame reached for him, Dieter's last breath was used for a plaintive moan, "*Mummi!*"

Each of the Mosquitos following Dilly Combes and Peter Osborne dropped two Napalm canisters on bunkers, machine gun nests, and mortar pits. Each then fired their four 20mm cannons and four Browning machine guns in between the Napalm fires. The plan was to expend all ammo in the target area. Combes fired the last of his cannon rounds just as he spotted a double column of red and yellow smoke on the sand, indicating the *Quinéville* turning point. Staying down at 100 feet, he turned the Mosquito to the right and, immediately, out over the Channel, climbing very slowly to 1500 feet. All of the Napalm-dropping Mosquitos returned safely to their bases, RAF Portreath and RAF Benson.

The *Flakpanzers* on the east shore of the Orne River

Leutnant Kaergel and his men were too far to the east to see or hear the Conga Line of the first ten twin-engined Mosquitos coming in at 100 feet from the Channel towards the town of *Vierville*. His radio net was a non-stop jumble of excited voices barking orders and confused questioners asking what was happening. Kaergel surmised from the chatter that fighter-bombers were attacking beach-front defenses between *Vierville* and the Cherbourg Peninsula. He couldn't see anything happening up that far up the beach.

Six miles behind Combe's aircraft, the second Mosquito section, which had exited Oxford Circus and headed south-southeast for the mouth of the Orne River, were approaching Sword, Juno, and Gold beaches. The *Flakpanzer* crews were completely taken by surprise as Flight Lieutenant David Campbell's Mosquito leading 89 following aircraft broke the horizon at 100 feet heading for their turn at the mouth of the Orne. A second Mosquito and then a third followed the same path. Kaergel ordered the *Flakpanzers* out from under the trees and the crews manned the two guns.

Campbell's Mosquito was already steering west up the beach when Kaergel and his gunners, still on the move, saw the first explosive Napalm fires. As they turned to the west, Mosquito Pilot RAF Flight Lieutenant Peter Osborne saw burning buildings along the beachfront. His observer, Sergeant Pilot Tom Castle called out, "That building on fire is the *Dauphine* Hotel. Our bunker target is just before the hotel." Osborne jinked to the right and then to the left, lining-up on the target.

By the time Kaergel's *Flakpanzers* had moved to where they had a clear view of the incoming planes, all the Mosquitos had passed and P-47s were now following the same track. "Fire!" yelled Kaergel and both gun crews opened-up, firing their twin Flak-38s. Unused to engaging aircraft at only 100 feet in altitude, their tracers showed their aim was too high and they corrected. P-47 Number 6 took a hit that broke an oil line and First Lieutenant Goldman's engine quickly began running rough. Short on options and time, Goldman remained cool, staying behind P-47 Number 5 and emptying his guns between the Napalm fires started a few minutes earlier by the Mosquitos. His guns now empty and his coughing engine approaching overheated levels, Goldman radioed,

"MAYDAY MAYDAY WOODFIRE SIX GOING DOWN. WILL DITCH IN THE CHANNEL."

Trailing black smoke, Goldman nursed the P-47 out over the Channel, steering for a spot without any small boats. The surface had four-foot swells and he made an OK water landing. Inflating his life vest, he climbed out on a wing and jumped in. The P-47 sank a minute later. Fifteen sailors with binoculars watched the ditching and

Goldman was picked-up, shivering with cold, less than ten minutes after going into the water.

HNoMS Nordkapp

Also watching through binoculars was *Løytnant*[175] Christian Nielson, skipper of HNoMS[176] Nordkapp. The Nordkapp, a small patrol vessel, was at the eastern edge of the invasion fleet, watching for German torpedo boats and submarines. Nielson spotted the tracers coming from Kaergel's *Flakpanzers*, out in the open.

Acting decisively on his own initiative, he ordered "All ahead full" and steered straight for the mouth of the Orne River. When a mile from shore, he slowed, steered east and ordered his 3-inch mount and 20mm *Oerlikon* guns to open fire at the *Flakpanzers*. The German gun crews, were fighting from roofless steel boxes good only for stopping small arms bullets but offered no protection against the Nordkapp's concentrated fire. Both *Flakpanzers* were silenced before they scored any further hits on the Conga Line aircraft. Everyone in both *Flak* crews was killed or wounded.

Remembering that the Germans had been occupying Norway and his home village since the Spring of 1940, *Konstabel* [177] Finn Ivorson on the Nordkapp muttered, "*Gud fordømte tyskerne!*" [178]

---

[175] Equivalent to Lieutenant Junior Grade in the USN.

[176] HNoMS: His Norwegian Majesty's Ship

[177] Equivalent to Leading Seaman

[178] "God damned Germans!"

The 24 Mosquitos were followed at half-mile intervals by the American P-47s, then the Canadian and New Zealand twin-engine Beaufighters. The Conga Line was progressing according to plan until New Zealander Flying Officer Liam Marsh jinked right to avoid going through a thick black cloud of Napalm smoke and then overcorrected when attempting to resume course behind the Beaufighter he was following.

The overcorrection brought his left wingtip into contact with the beachfront bluff in a shower of sparks and sand. Marsh had already expended all his ammunition and immediately focused on trying to stabilize his aircraft. He discovered that he had lost four feet of his left wing and, with it, the left aileron. Other than some vibration caused by jagged pieces of the wing flapping in the airstream, the airplane seemed controllable. Marsh kept his Conga Line position but was forced to make flat turns, using only his rudder. He made it back to RAF Langham with the rest of his Number 489 Squadron mates, who thereafter dubbed him "Kamikazi Marsh."

The Beaufighters were followed by the American P-38s, all strafing exposed German firing positions with cannon and machine guns. Next in trail were ten RAF B-25 "Mitchells" and ten American B-26s. All forward-firing cannons in the noses of the B-25s and B-26s plus all their tail guns fired at the mortar pits and machine gun nests. On four of the B-26s, the left waist guns were replaced by cameras. Motion picture cameras on two aircraft and photographers with still cameras on the other two. Left waist guns on the remaining B-26s and on all the B-25s fired as well.

 RCAF Flying Officer Keith Morton held the nose of his Beaufighter on one of four artillery casemates on the bluffs at *Longues-sur-Mer*. He described later, at debriefing, that he could see his cannon rounds striking at the wide open gun port with many going inside. Morton's observation was confirmed by the pilot following him that there was an explosion inside the casemate that blew its 155mm gun out onto the ground. Intelligence later concluded the explosion was artillery ammunition going off inside after being hit by Morton's cannon fire.

Other returning pilots reported seeing very few people in the target area. A few were seen on building rooftops in the waterfront towns and a few others running toward bunkers, unfortunately into a hail of fire from the Close Air Support aircraft.

As the B-25s and B-26s were into their firing passes, Stu and US Army Lieutenant Colonel Dan Hopewell, on board the B-24, both saw through binoculars that landing craft were very close to Omaha and Utah beaches. Inside the bomber, with the left waist window open, it was too noisy to talk and hear. Hopewell, the Beach Liaison Officer, looking at Stu, drew his pointing finger across his own throat, gesturing, "Cut" or "End it." Stu nodded emphatically and gave Hopewell a thumbs up sign, immediately pressing the "Push-to-Talk" button on his microphone to release the ten reserve Mosquitos.

"JELLYROLL - JELLYROLL - THIS IS FAST EDDIE.

BLOWTORCH – REPEAT - BLOWTORCH

AUTHENTICATION –CHARLIE PETER HOW – REPEAT - CHARLIE PETER HOW"

Stu and Morton watched, fascinated, as swarms of infantry poured out onto the beach, moving from German-placed obstacle to obstacle, pausing only briefly before moving towards the sea wall. Isolated explosions on the sand knocked down small numbers of men. Grim-faced, Lieutenant Colonel Morton scribbled on a pad, "Land mines," and showed it to Stu.

As the B-24 flew westward, Morton poked Stu's arm and pointed toward the *Pointe du Hoc*, which was pouring thick black smoke toward the southeast. Using only his good right eye through one side of the binoculars, Stu was able to see Rangers climbing the cliff face.

Next, US Navy Lieutenant Tim Palmer called Stu on the Intercom. "Beefstew, the Fleet wants to know when we will move out. They want to be ready for any gunfire support requests coming from troops ashore."

"Guess it's time for us to head for home. Good job everybody."

Stu next released the P-51s overhead flying Combat Air Patrol to look for targets of opportunity. Over the Intercom, he told the pilot, Captain Earl Clark, "Skipper, we're done here; let's head for Greenham."

The northward view of the 32 mobile anti-aircraft guns that Rommel had repositioned two-to-three miles behind the beaches was blocked by the height of the bluffs. None could see any of the Conga Line aircraft flying at 100 feet and never fired a shot at them.

Operation BOOKMARK: the Conga Line Aircraft

Top Row, left to right: De Havilland Mosquito; Republic P-47; Bristol Beaufighter

Second Row, left to right: Lockheed P-38; B-25; B-26

Third Row, left to right: P-51, Consolidated B-24 (the Airborne Command Post)

[For the BOOKMARK Operation, the wings of all the aircraft would have been painted with white "Invasion Stripes" as seen on the B-26 and P-51, above. The stripes were for identification by anti-aircraft forces in the UK].

CHAPTER 48

Allied Troops Ashore in Normandy

As the Higgins Boats dropped their ramps several yards short of the sand of Omaha Beach, the men of the 29th Infantry Division poured out, waded ashore, and began moving toward the crossed-iron obstacles that littered the beach. Instinctively pausing behind what little protection the obstacles provided, those first ashore saw black, smoky fires burning all along the sea wall and bluffs before them. No hostile fire was coming their way so small groups cautiously, moved forward, briefly pausing at successive obstacles. Someone stepped on a land mine and four men went down. Everybody froze momentarily, looking in the direction of the explosion. Frantic calls for a "Medic" were mixed with orders from officers and NCOs to "Move up!"

As troops began to reach the sea wall, single soldiers were sent right up to bunker walls, mortar pits, and machine gun nests while their squad mates provided covering fire. Their task: throw hand grenades into the silent emplacements from which enemy fire had been expected. In short order, all the fortified German positions were declared "cleared." The "second wave" of landing craft started reaching the shoreline. General Norman Cota was with them.

As the men moved past the silent German defense positions, numerous curious soldiers peered inside the bunkers at the tangled piles of corpses. The Combat Photographers and Intelligence troops documented the absence of any German troops, machine guns, or mortars in the outdoor positions, which were burned black by the napalm. Some of the bunkers were surrounded by piles of dismembered corpses, obviously hit by large artillery explosions.

Occasional German artillery projectiles hit the beach, causing small numbers of casualties. As soon as Allied troops started moving off the beach, German artillery positions were plotted and naval gunfire support was requested; several of the German batteries were silenced. The rest were overrun by Allied advances.

Up on the seawall above Omaha Beach, General Cota first observed with satisfaction large numbers of the 29th Division moving off the sand and inland and then looked back at the beach and the few, who had been killed. The thought crossed his mind that it could have been far worse. He felt in his breast pocket for a cigar, put it between his teeth. "God bless you Beefstew!" he thought to himself as he flagged-down a jeep to take him forward to the division's lead elements.

ANNEX A

CITATION TO ACCOMPANY THE AWARD OF

THE LEGION OF MERIT

TO

FRANZ S. RITTERSBERG, III

Captain Franz S. Rittersberg, III, 66963, United States Army Air Forces, distinguished himself by exceptionally meritorious achievement as planner and developer of innovative Airborne Command and Control and Close Air Support tactics for the Operation OVERLORD invasion of enemy-occupied France in June 1944, while assigned to Supreme Headquarters of the Allied Expeditionary Force (SHAEF). As a member of the headquarters planning staff, Captain Rittersberg identified a shortcoming in previous amphibious landings that contributed to high friendly casualty rates and conceived new and untried corrections for which he gained approval at the highest levels of SHAEF. Captain Rittersberg then flew as the Airborne Controller for D-Day Close Air Support operations involving 110 aircraft of four Allied air forces. Allied infantry division commanders attribute the lower than expected casualty numbers on invasion beaches to the timely neutralization of enemy fortifications and personnel resulting from the tactics conceived and directed by Captain Rittersberg. Through his distinctive accomplishments, Captain Rittersberg reflected great credit upon himself, the United States Army Air Forces and the War Department.

18 July 1944

Official: Dwight D. Eisenhower

Dwight D. Eisenhower
General, US Army
Supreme Allied Commander

ANNEX B

EPILOGUE

The Actual Historical Characters

- General Dwight D. Eisenhower became the 34th President of the US.
- General Omar Bradley became Chief of Staff of the US Army.
- Lieutenant General George Patton distinguished himself as the most effective Army general of the war – all warring nations considered. He was killed in an automobile accident in Germany shortly after the war. Conspiracy theories about the fatal accident continue.
- Brigadier General Norman Cota actually went ashore at Omaha Beach in the 2nd Wave. The movie, *The Longest Day* created a myth by having him land with the 1st wave. But Cota's outstanding leadership on D-Day earned him a second star and command of the 28th Infantry Division – originally of the federalized Pennsylvania National Guard.
- Field Marshall Bernard Montgomery was actually a thorn in Eisenhower's side during the planning phase of Operation OVERLORD. He later devised the over-ambitious MARKET-GARDEN thrust into the Netherlands, which failed. After the war, Montgomery

was Commander of the British Army of the Rhine and then Deputy Supreme Commander of NATO.
- Air Chief Marshall Trafford Leigh-Mallory continued serving as the SHAEF Air Forces Commander until he died in a plane crash in November 1944.
- *Feldmarschall* Erwin Rommel was implicated in the plot to assassinate Hitler and was compelled by the SS to commit suicide.
- General Erich Marcks was killed when his staff car was strafed six days after the Normandy landings.

The Fictitious Characters

- Stu "Beefstew" Rittersberg moved to Versailles, France with SHAEF after D-Day, transferring to the Air Forces Planning Office. Stu and his father visited Le Havre after the fighting had moved toward the east in the winter of 1944. Le Havre was still in German hands in September 1944 and Allied Operation ASTONIA was launched to capture the city, which Hitler had ordered held "to the last man." The German commander proposed a brief truce to allow French civilians to evacuate the city but the Allies refused, instead subjecting the port and city to heavy aerial and naval bombardment, which killed over 2000 French civilians but only 19 Germans. (*https:// en.wikipedia.org/wiki/Operation_Astonia*). Fictitious Stu and his father found Maggi's house at 88 *Rue Moliere* and all the neighboring houses totally destroyed. The Church of St Jean Baptiste had many broken windows. In the churchyard they found *Père* Antoine's resting place and in a corner of the yard, a plaque on the wall listing the dead from the "Spanish Flu" pandemic of

1919. Stu's mother was listed as "Marguerite Renier, *Infirmiere*." It was an emotional visit for father and son, who left flowers. Frank picked up a fistful of earth from the churchyard corner. He kept it near him in a small glass bottle. Stu realized aloud that all his French forbears were gone. Frank made a generous contribution for restoration of the church's windows.

- Stu's father went back to Harrisburg and the Pennsylvania National Guard and retired in 1946. Stu stayed in the Army and transferred to the new US Air Force in 1947. He was the Air Force's authority on Airborne Command and Control and Airborne Command Posts, writing the early doctrine on the subject. Stu was an Adjunct Professor at the US Military Academy and the Air Force Academy. He retired in 1972 as a Major General. He married and had 2 children, Marguerite and Franz IV.

- Reg Childs, Stu's office partner at SHAEF, was posted to RAF Headquarters after D-Day. He was demobbed[179] in late 1946 and returned to Wales for a career in railroad scheduling and management.

- LCDR George Christianson persuaded his boss to recommend him for assignment as a Gunnery Officer on a ship that would participate in the D-Day landings. Christianson was on the Destroyer USS Glennon, which struck a mine while shelling German positions ashore on D-Day. Disabled and unable to move, the Glennon was hit by a German Coast Artillery shore battery near Quinéville. Christianson and 25 of his crewmen were killed. (Factual but Christianson is fictional).

---

[179] Demobilised or discharged in Brit-speak

- Bernard Perrier. Continued teaching in Barfleur. Moving quickly after D-Day, General Charles de Gaulle entered Paris and the Communists in the *Résistance* had no chance to seize power. Disillusioned with post-war labor strife, Perrier emigrated to Quebec in 1948.
- Etiennne Aguillon returned to full-time fishing. With the surplus minesweeper he bought after the war, he operated two fishing boats.
- Josephene Aguillon – reopened the fish store with her sister-in-law. In 1949, they opened a successful waterfront seafood restaurant on *Quai Henri Chardon*. Josephine became active in the labor union, *Confédération générale du travail unitaire* (CGTU),
- Yuri Grigorevich continued working for the Soviet GRU and spent several years in Bucharest at the Soviet Embassy after the Communists took power in the Soviet Bloc. He remained friendly with Anna till her death.
- Bruno and Anna Roeder lost all 3 sons: one on the battleship Tirpitz, when it was bombed by the RAF; one in a U-Boat lost in the Atlantic; and Dieter at Normandy. Mainz was an important rail hub in the southern Rhineland and thus became a target for Allied bombers. The Third Army also successfully crossed the Rhine near Mainz and Bruno and Anna became refugees fleeing the fighting. Retreating German infantry sheltered in the abandoned Roeder farmhouse and barn, which were totally destroyed.
- Pierre Fermier, the Trashman survived the invasion as did his horse, Leo. They lived out their days in a free France.
- **Sergeant** Bohdan Glushenko the Ukrainian, was killed by Allied artillery. He never fired a shot at the Allies.

ANNEX C

GROUND TRUTH, ENDNOTES,
and PHOTO CREDITS

The author welcomes comments, questions, and alternate views. Contact Bill Grayson at *sheffordpress@ earthlink.net*.

In some of the End Notes I refer to myself as "I." Referring to myself as "the author" seems too stuffy.

This is a work of fiction with a dose of Alternative History (AH) at its end. Robert Woods/Standout Books, an AH coach instructs: *"AH fiction is judged on two criteria. The first is how believable the reader finds the story in comparison to real life – could it, as suggested, actually have happened? The second is how believably the events of the story lead into each other."* I tried to conform to these two criteria.

Ground Truth

In the earth sciences, actual field checks to determine "Ground Truth" are performed at subject locations to confirm observations made via photography, radar, or other remote sensors. The term "Ground Truth" has been adapted routinely for use in military exercises to distinguish between what is real versus what has been written into a notional script. Thus, a military exercise scenario might include, as "Ground Truth," an actual road leading to an actual town, while the notional script might place "imaginary" enemy fortifications on either side of the road. I use the term "Ground Truth" is in *Beefstew* to differentiate the factual record from the book's fiction and alternative history.

END NOTES and PHOTO CREDITS

Chapter 1 - 1943 in England - Stu Rittersberg

Stu Rittersberg and Reg Childs are fictitious characters inserted into the actual history of the real 31st Fighter Group. The 31st was based at Selfridge, flying P-39s and did deploy to England without their aircraft in 1942. The Group actually converted to P-38s and did fly in support of the British/Canadian raid at Dieppe.

Stu's father, Franz S. Rittersberg Jr. is a fictitious character. ETOUSA was an actual organization in England – a forerunner of SHAEF.

Photo Credits: P-38, P-39 – US Army

Chapter 2 - Young Franz Steuben Rittersberg, Jr. (Stu's Father)

Dwight Eisenhower was on the 1912 West Point football team and actually did injure his knee tackling Jim Thorpe during the Army-Carlyle game on November 9th. That injury did actually end Ike's football playing but he did coach football for many years thereafter.

During the early days of World War I, Winston Churchill did advocate the use of "land battleships," which were realized as tanks.

Photo Credit: Jim Thorpe – Library of Congress.

Chapter 3 - June 1917, Seeing Franz Jr, off to France

Although a majority were adamantly opposed to US entry into World War I, many Americans actually were furious with Germany over the Lusitania sinking, the massive sabotage explosion at the "Black Tom" docks in New York harbor, and the perfidious *"Zimmerman Telegram."*

Photo Credit: The Army uniform picture is adapted from one at the Fort Meade Museum.

Chapter 4 - In France, September 12, 1918

The US Army actually used French *Renault* tanks and the US' first tank battle was at St. Mihiel in September 1918. The chapter's description of the *Renault's* limited performance is actual.

The Number 1 Field Hospital was actually at Etretat, France. The location had been chosen by the British Army for its proximity to the port of Le Havre, a short evacuation distance for wounded troops back to England.

Lt. Colonel George Patton was actually shot through his left leg and was hospitalized. His treatment at Etretat is fictitious but he was actually promoted to Colonel while hospitalized.

Nurse Marguerite Renier is a fictitious character. I have given her the name of a French pen-pal I had while in high school. The photo of a nurse is from the National Archives.

Senator Jim Davis of Pennsylvania was an actual person. He did visit France in 1918 as chairman of the Loyal Order of Moose War Relief Commission. Davis' visit to Etretat is fictitious.

Photo Credit: Senator Davis – Library of Congress

Chapter 5 - Marguerite (Maggi) Renier

France's first battle of World War I was at Stonne but all the events and characters of the chapter are fictitious. Franz Jr's ancestry is likewise fictitious.

Chapter 6 - Christmas 1918, Etretat Hospital

The chapter is totally fictitious but the description of the town of Etretat and the white chalk cliffs are actual.

Photo Credit: Hotel Place – France Tourism

Chapter 7 - December 1918, Maggi: Back in Le Havre

The chapter and all its characters are totally fictitious but inserted into the "Spanish Flu" epidemic, which actually occurred during the chapter's timeframe and killed over 20 million people, world-wide.

Concerning the likelihood that Maggi would have yielded and become pregnant during her first coupling, it is well-established that a woman's libido peaks during her most fertile time. Perhaps, Maggi's ovulation, the champagne, and her love for Frank led to her suggestion that they go outside.

Père Antoine's priestly order, the Congregation of the Sons of Mary Immaculate (FMI), is real.

Chapter 8 - December 1919, The Search for Frank, Etretat Field Hospital

The *Eglise St. Jean Baptiste* in Le Havre and St. Anne's Church in Annapolis are both real but the chapter and all its characters are fictitious. The 305th Tank Brigade was real at Camp Meade, Maryland during the chapter's timeframe.

Chapter 9 - Camp Meade, Maryland

Colonel George Patton and Major Dwight Eisenhower were actually stationed together at Camp Meade, working on the first US-built tank – the Mark VIII *Liberty*. They were actually neighbors on 4th Street after Ike and Mamie Eisenhower moved into quarters from nearby Laurel, Maryland. The Eisenhowers had a 3-year old son, Doud, nicknamed "Icky." The chapter's events and other characters are fictitious.

Photo Credits: Liberty Tank, Patton, Eisenhower – Fort Meade Museum; Bea Patton and Mamie Eisenhower – Wiki Commons; Eisenhower Family – Dwight D Eisenhower Library

Chapter 10 - April 1920, Understanding Franz Rittersberg, Sr. – Stu's Grandfather

Dennis Michie is a historic character, who pioneered football at West Point in 1890. He actually was killed in action in Cuba during the Spanish-American War in 1898. Michie Field, later Michie Stadium is named for him.

In 1916, Lieutenant George Patton actually rode with Pershing into Mexico in pursuit of Pancho Villa. James J. Davis was an actual US Senator and prominent Loyal Order of Moose organizer. Beatrice Patton, George's wife lived with him in Officer's Quarters at Camp Meade. Patton actually home-brewed beer and Eisenhower actually home-distilled gin.

The chapter's events and all its other characters are fictitious.

Photo Credits Buick and 1913 football team - Library of Congress; MV Radnor – National Archives.

Chapter 11 - March 1920, The Fetch Trip

In 1920, the SS Radnor actually sailed as an ocean liner after having served as a troopship during the First World War.

Eric Wood is an actual character and the chapter's description of his World War I service is true. All other characters and events in the chapter are fictitious.

St. John Baptiste Church is actually at 139 *Rue Theophile Gautier* in Le Havre

Photo Credits: Buick and 1913 football team - Library of Congress; MV Radnor – National Archives; Church of St Jean – France Tourism; Pram – Ebay; RMS Olympic - Library of Congress.

Chapter 12 - April 1920, New York

Completely fictitious.

Photo Credit: Buick - Library of Congress.

Chapter 13 - May 1920, Camp Meade, Maryland

Colonel George Patton was actually transferred to Fort Meyer. Radio station WTAW actually broadcast the first college football game heard nationwide between Texas U and Mechanical College of Texas.

Icky Eisenhower actually died from Scarlet Fever on January 2, 1921.

Dwight Eisenhower was actually transferred from Camp Meade to Panama in 1921.

The remainder of the chapter is fictitious.

Photo Credit: Tank Corps – Fort Meade Museum

Chapter 14 - 1922 Frank joins the Pennsylvania National Guard

Discussion of the 28th Infantry Division is factual.

The books and movies enjoyed by fictitious "Fuzzy" are historically true and from the period discussed.

Carson Long in Pennsylvania is actually the nation's oldest preparatory boarding school and military academy.

The Class B Harrisburg Senators actually played at Island Field. The Philadelphia Phillies actually played at the Baker Bowl. On July 11, the New York Giants actually beat the Phillies 23 to 5 in the first game of a doubleheader.

The books Fuzzy read by Antoine de Saint-Exupéry are real and from the period covered in the chapter.

The Thomas Jefferson quote, "*Chaque homme a deux patries: la sienne et la France,*" is factual.

The remainder of the chapter is fictitious.

Photo Credit: Curtiss Jenny – Library of Congress

Chapter 15 - The US Enters World War II

The 28th Infantry Division, a part of the Pennsylvania National Guard, was federalized after Pearl Harbor and was sent to Louisiana for training.

Dwight Eisenhower was named Commander of the Allied Expeditionary Force in North Africa and did go to Gibraltar to plan the invasion with British forces.

The remainder of the chapter is fictitious.

Chapter 16 - August 1942, Chemical Warfare Research at Porton Down, UK

British Chemical warfare studies during World War II were actually conducted at the Experimental Research

Ground at Porton Down but all of the chapter and its characters are fictitious.

Chapter 17 - September 1942, Joseph Stalin

Although Stalin had signed a pact with Hitler that permitted the German conquest of Poland, Stalin was surprised by Hitler's "Operation Barbarossa" and his massive invasion of the USSR. Stalin repeatedly did press Churchill and Roosevelt to open a "second front" to draw some German forces out of the western USSR.

Communists actually did play a leading role in the French *Résistance*. Stalin actually valued the efforts of the *Résistance* and actually hoped for a Communist France after a successful Allied invasion.

The chapter's events and all its other characters are fictitious.

Photo Credit: Stalin – Library of Congress

Chapter 18 – 1942, France and Josephine Aguillon

The chapter's events and all its characters are fictitious.

Photo Credit: Fishing boat – author.

Chapter 19 – 1942, *Soldat* Dieter Roeder

The chapter's events and all its characters are fictitious.

"Be a man" is what my father said to me at the airport as I left for Vietnam in 1966.

Chapter 20 - 1943, Yuri Gregorevich Egorov

During World War II, the Soviet Black Sea Fleet actually had a submarine base at Poti.

"*Sprut*" commemorates the name of the Soviet submarine featured in the1966 United Artists film, "The Russians Are Coming."

Romanian General Ion Antenescu actually led a *coup d'état* that toppled Romania's neutral government and he actually declared allegiance to Hitler's Germany.

The chapter's other events and all its characters are fictitious.

Photo Credits: Railcars – German *Bundesarchiv*

Chapter 21 –Pierre Fermier, The Trashman

The chapter's events and all its characters are fictitious.

Chapter 22 – 1943, Ukrainians in German Uniforms

During World War II, many Ukrainians actually did welcome the Germans as "liberators" from harsh Soviet rule. In 1943, the independent Ukrainian People's Army (UPA) was simultaneously anti-German and anti-USSR in its quest for sovereign statehood. Many Ukrainians were absorbed by the German army, the "*Heer*," and were shipped west, away from their home country, to serve in non-combat roles.

An "*Ost*" (East) Battalion was actually part of the German 726th Infantry Division, at Normandy but the chapter's events and all its characters are fictitious.

Chapter 23 - February 1944, *Chateau La Roche Guyon*, 40mi n of Paris

Chateau La Roche Guyon actually was the headquarters of *Feldmarschall* Erwin Rommel.

Colonel Anton Staubwasser was actually Rommel's Chief of Intelligence. The Allied strengths described by Staubwasser are factual.

In 1944, it was the consensus among senior German officials that an Allied invasion would be attempted, most probably at the *Pas de Calais*.

General Erich Marcks, Commander of the 84th Korps in Normandy actually dissented, believing that Normandy would be the main Allied invasion objective. His part in the chapter is fictitious.

Generalleutnant Wilhelm Richter was actually Commander of the 716th Infantry Division based in the town of La Folie-Couvrechef, just north of Caen but his part in the chapter is fictitious.

The Germans actually did believe an invasion would occur during a Full Moon/New Moon period.

Colonel Walter Korfes was actually Commander of Grenadier-Regiment 726. His headquarters was actually in the *Château de Sully*.

Lieutenant Edmund Bauch was actually a Company Commander in Grenadier-Regiment 726 but his part in the chapter is fictitious.

SHAEF actually studied the structure of sand at the Normandy beaches. British commandos actually went ashore to collect sand samples and take them back in England.

Otherwise, the chapter's events are fictitious.

Two of Delaware's towers

Concerning the mixing of beach sand with cement for beachfront structures, in 1940-41, the US Army Coast Artillery Corps constructed 15 Fire Control Towers along the Atlantic in Delaware and New Jersey using beach sand – because it was right there in unlimited quantity. At the time of construction, the towers were expected to last only 20 years but were all still standing at the time of this writing. I suspect but have no evidence that the Germans used beach sand in constructing Rommel's "Atlantic Wall."

Photo Credits: Chateau La Roche Guyon – France Tourism; General Marcks and Kubelwagen – German Bundesarchiv; Chateau de Sully – France Tourism; Two Delaware towers – author.

Chapter 24 - October 1943 in Algeria

While stationed in Algeria, General Eisenhower actually had his headquarters in the St. George Hotel in Algiers. He actually sent Generals Bradley and Cota ahead to London to start organizing for the invasion of France.

Frank Rittersberg is a fictitious character.

Photo Credits: Eisenhower and Pierced Steel Planking –
US Army.

Chapter 25 - 1943 - *Leutnant* Edmund Bauch, 726th Grenadier-Regiment

The chapter's events and all its characters other than
Bauch are fictitious but Bauch's part in the chapter is
fictitious.

Photo Credit: Mont St Michel – author.

Chapter 26 - January 1944, A Normandy Beach, Battle Station Drill

The 7.92mm MG-42 Machine Gun was mounted on a
Lafette 42 tripod. The tripod's *Tiefenfeuerautomat* feature
is factual.

However, the chapter's events and all its characters are
fictitious.

Photo Credit: MG-42 – German *Bundesarchiv*.

Chapter 27 - January 1944, Stu's Planning Assignment

SHAEF Headquarters was actually at Camp Griffiss in
Bushy Park, west of London.

The Yank's playful epithet "Dirty Duck" commemorates
the Black Swan in Shefford, Bedfordshire, called the
"Dirty Duck" by USAF members stationed at nearby RAF
Chicksands.

Operation JUBILEE was actually the August 1940 failed invasion of Dieppe. Over 6000 infantry did go ashore and 60% were very quickly killed, wounded or captured. The British First Sea Lord, Sir Dudley Pound, wouldn't risk a cruiser or battleship without air superiority. Next, most of the pre-landing aerial bombardment was curtailed so as not to kill French civilians.

Canadian Major Allen Glenn of the Calgary Tank Regiment actually wrote the "worst terrain" report for a tracked vehicle. Loose stones on the beach at Dieppe actually broke their treads and all the Canadian tanks were destroyed at water's edge.

The beach resort town of *Vierville sur Mer* actually overlooks Omaha Beach.

However, the chapter's events and all its characters are fictitious.

Photo Credit: Black Swan Hotel – author.

Chapter 28 - February 1944, Stu Sees Aircraft

During World War II, German bomber pilots intentionally "desynchronized" their engines, incorrectly believing that technique would degrade British directional sound equipment.

The chapter's events are fictitious.

Chapter 29 - February 1944, Stu's Epiphany

Eddie Rickenbacker's World War I memoir, *Fighting the Flying Circus,* documents Rickenbacker's pioneering airborne command and control while flying above his squadron's formation.

The chapter's events are fictitious.

Chapter 30 - February 1944, General Cota's Tuesday Staff Meeting

The chapter presents a basically accurate Allied assessment of German defenses at Normandy.

The Atlantic Wall fortifications were actually made of thick, steel-reinforced concrete. I have walked the German line of bunkers at several Normandy beach locations, observing deep shell craters remaining from the D-Day naval bombardment but the absence of any bunkers blown apart by air-dropped bombs or naval projectiles. The chapter's description of protective shelters for German troops manning the beach defenses is actual and more than 1000 were constructed along the full length of the Atlantic Wall. An article in the January 2018 issue of *Military History* magazine includes a drawing and brief discussion of the Normandy *Gruppenständ* shelters.

General Norman Cota actually tried to persuade General Eisenhower and the SHAEF staff that the odds of a successful landing at Normandy during daylight were greatly unfavorable. He recommended landings at night.

Professor Frederick Shotton of Birmingham University actually performed the sand analysis.

Rear Admiral A.G. Kirk and Captain (later Rear Admiral) D.P. Moon actually served on the SHAEF staff but their appearance in this chapter is fictitious.

Other characters and discussions in the chapter are fictional but Navy actually did beat Army 6 to zero in 1912.

Chapter 31 - February 1944, Questions for George Christenson

The chapter is totally fictitious.

Chapter 32 - February 1944 - John O'Rourke visits Ben Cooley

The chapter is totally fictitious.

Chapter 33 – The Whirlpool

The chapter is totally fictitious.

Chapter 34 - Stu Briefs General Cota

Reg Childs' introductory assessment is historically accurate " . . .casualties have been highest where the naval bombardment's results were less effective than expected or where there was no naval bombardment either to achieve surprise or to avoid civilian casualties. Dieppe – North Africa – Sicily. In the Pacific, Guadalcanal – Attu – and, a couple of months ago, Tarawa. And in none of those costly invasions were enemy defenders so solidly dug-in and fortified as what we are facing in Normandy."

Colonel Frank Hill was actually CO of the 31st Fighter Group in 1943.

General Cota is real but Lt. Col. Harmon and his conversation with Cota are fictitious.

Photo Credits: General Cota – US Army.

Chapter 35 - Air Forces Challenges to BOOKMARK

RAF Air Marshall Sir Trafford Leigh-Mallory was actually Commander-in-Chief of the Allied Expeditionary Air Force at SHAEF Headquarters. He actually resisted the use of heavy and medium bombers in a tactical sense against German beachfront defenses, preferring to use the bombers against strategic targets on D-Day.

I surmise that he really would have been a tough sell concerning the diversion of 110 tactical aircraft from already-planned D-Day operations but the chapter's events are fictitious.

Chapter 36 - Cota and Bradley

The chapter is totally fictitious.

Photo Credits: ACM Leigh-Mallory – RAF; General Bradley – US Army; Ike and FM Montgomery – Library of Congress.

Chapter 37 - February 1944 - Navy and RAF Conditions and Demands

The chapter remembers Eric Watt, RAF "Y" Service at RAF Chicksands during World War II.

The fictitious character "Gary Williamson's" name is an anagram of the author's.

The 34th Bomb **Group** was actually based at RAF Mendelsham, flying B-24s. "Iowa Girl" is a fictitious B-24 name.

BC-458A transmitters, BC-348H receivers, and LP-21 Loop fairings were actual aircraft radio components in 1944.

Chapter 38 - At The *Hôtel de la Plage*

The hotel is fictional.

The Soviet Army's Military-Chemical Administration (*VOKhIMU*) was an actual organization during World War II.

The four "color" plans assigned to the French *Résistance* are historically factual.

The chapter's scenario and characters are fictitious.

Photo Credits: Pharmacy - author

Chapter 39 - The Plan: Operation BOOKMARK

The chapter is fiction but uses actual US, British, Canadian, and New Zealander Air Force squadrons, their aircraft types, and bases from 1944. All the characters are fictitious except for the reference to Eddie Rickenbacker.

In inventing the list of aircraft types making up the fictitious Conga Line, I put Mosquitos up front in recognition of the reputation established by RAF/RAAF/RNZAF Mosquitos for great accuracy in striking individual target buildings from very low altitudes.

The first-ever tactical use of air-dropped napalm actually occurred in 1944 from RAF Mosquitos. Even though it was available, the first use, however, wasn't at Normandy on D-Day. **No one thought of it!**

The Ploesti anecdote included in the chapter is historically accurate.

For some obscure reason, General Omar Bradley, Commander of the 1ˢᵗ Army, refused to draw upon earlier US amphibious landing experience in the Pacific Theater. US Army Major General Charles H. Corbett was specifically transferred by Chief of Staff General George Marshall from the Pacific to England to contribute his experience and understanding of the causes of high landing casualties. W. Murray, writing in *War, Strategy and Military Effectiveness* (ISBN 978-110761-4383), asserts that Bradley snubbed Corbett and derided Pacific island invasions as "Bush League." Also, Bradley actually did have the pre-landing naval barrage at Omaha Beach shortened from 40 to 20 minutes. I have researched unsuccessfully to discover Bradley's rationale and would appreciate learning from any reader who finds it. Numerous on-line sources document Bradley's curtailment without rationale. One source is *https://www.quora.com/On-D-Day-June-6-1944*. In this fictional story, General Bradley might not have had Stu and Reg Childs waste their time on "bush league" stuff.

Photo Credits: Eddie Rickenbacker – National Archives.

Chapter 40 - Stu's Flight Physical

The chapter and its characters are fictitious.

An eye chart for optometrists' offices is for sale on the Internet. The 20-20 line on that for-sale chart is actually "D-E-F-P-O-T-E-C." (*http://cdna.allaboutvision.com/i/eye-test/eye-charts-330x311@2x.png*)

Chapter 41 - 12 May 1944, Stu Visits Greenham Common

By sending Stu to RAF Greenham Common in a UC-46, I took the opportunity to remember bandleader Major Glenn Miller, who disappeared over the English Channel on December 15, 1944 in a UC-46.

Colonel Wackwitz actually was CO of the 34th Bomb Group in 1944. All other characters and events in the chapter are fictitious.

Photo Credits: UC-46 and B-24 – US Army.

Chapter 42 – May 1944, Franceville, *Flakpanzers*

The Germans actually used tanks fitted with anti-aircraft guns but the chapter is totally fictitious. The German *Flak-38* was a commonly-used anti-aircraft weapon not only along Rommel's "Atlantic Wall" but on-board ships of the *Kriegsmarine* as well. A twin-barreled Flak-38, recovered from sunken submarine U853, has been restored and preserved in the museum at Fort Miles, Delaware in Cape Henlopen State Park. This is certainly the world's best example of the formidable weapon that seriously challenged Allied forces during World War II. Readers interested in Germany's "Atlantic Wall" may also find interesting a US counterpart at the Coast Artillery Museum in Delaware's Cape Henlopen State Park.

Twin Flak-38 mount from U853

Photo Credit: Flak-38 in Fort Miles Museum – author.

Chapter 43 – June 1944, The BBC *en Français*

Much of the chapter, including message texts, the BBC presence in Bedford, and routing of broadcasts via RAF Chicksands, is factual but all the characters are fictitious.

The BBC information, information about Bedford, the RAF Chicksands antennas, the increase in messages to the French *Résistance*, and all the message texts but one are genuine and were transmitted from the BBC studio in Bedford. The one fictitious message is *"Simone a perdu un gant rouge."*

The Bedford Swan Hotel on the Great Ouse River Embankment does date from 1794 and is the author's favourite.

Photo Credits - Bedford Swan Hotel and Chicksands Priory – author; Cyclist – German Bundesarchiv

Chapter 44 – *Erdbeerenfest*

Erdbeerenfest (Strawberry Festival) is actually observed all over Germany in springtime.

The chapter's events and characters are fictitious.

Photo Credits: Food - author

Chapter 45 – 5 June / Full Moon

The chapter's events and characters are fictitious.

Photo Credit: *Flakpanzer* in Normandy, 1944 - German *Bundesdarchiv.*

Chapter 46 - Just after Midnight, 6 June

The chapter inserts fictitious characters and building names into an event timeline that is historically accurate. The exception to the timeline is that hundreds of German machine gun and mortar crews, artillerymen, and riflemen plus their weapons were protected by their reinforced concrete *gruppenstands* and actually survived the aerial bombing and naval bombardment, which failed to produce intended results. During the actual period between the lifting of the naval bombardment and the arrival on shore of the landing craft, there was sufficient time for German troops and their guns to get to their mostly intact Battle Stations, ready to open fire as Allied troops "hit the beach." 4414 Allied men died. Many thousand more were wounded.

Over 3000 French civilians were actually killed on D-Day by bombs dropped from Allied aircraft and projectiles fired by Allied ships.

Photo Credit: HNoMS Nordkapp – Imperial War Museum.

Chapter 47 - 6 June 1944, the D-Day Landings and Operation BOOKMARK

German anti-aircraft batteries were actually deployed in large numbers just south of the Normandy beaches and did fire thousands of rounds at the transport aircraft carrying Allied paratroopers and/or towing gliders at altitudes below 10,000 feet. Many were actually shot down. The chapter's specific events and characters are, however, totally fictitious.

Photo Credit: In a Higgins Boat – US Navy Historical and Heritage Command, the fleet – National Archives; Conga Line aircraft – Mosquito and Beaufighter – Imperial War Museum; P-47, P-38, B-25, B-26, P-51, B-24 – US Army.

Chapter 48 - 6 June 1944, Allied Troops Ashore in Normandy

The chapter's characters and events are totally fictitious. Much of the fundamental OVERLORD planning and choice of dates for the beach landings did center on a full moon and the highest tides. Actually, Rommel's beach obstacles, designed to tear open the bottoms of landing craft, led to Allied changes in the plan and the troop-carrying Higgins Boats actually dropped their ramps and soldiers entered the water many yards from the beach. Troops were loaded with back-packs, utility belts, hand-held weapons and equipment weighing between 60 to

100 pounds. Large numbers of men jumped from landing craft into water too deep to stand and many drowned.

Photo Credit: Beach obstacles – German *Bundesarchiv*.

ANNEX A – Stu's Legion of Merit

If an actual Stu had conceived, sold, and led an actual Operation BOOKMARK, it is highly likely that he would have been awarded the Legion of Merit. To make the certificate look authentic, I used my own USAF Serial Number to avoid inadvertently misusing anyone else's.

A SOBERING NOTE ABOUT UNINTENDED CIVILIAN CASUALTIES

At the time of this writing in 2017, US Armed Forces engaged in combat in the Middle East and Africa are controlled by the Department of Defense's *Law of War Manual*, a 1200 page document promulgated by the DoD's General Counsel. The main thrust of the Manual is the reduction of civilian casualties through judicious choices of targets, weapons, and timing. "Proportionality" is the instructive guidance provided by the DoD. Under the heading, "Proportionality in Conducting Attacks," the Manual grapples with a cardinal rule in the laws of war: "Commanders must refrain from carrying out a strike that is expected to result in excessive civilian casualties compared to the concrete military advantage to be gained."

From time-to-time, in interpreting the Manual, an actual small number of "allowable" collateral casualties is imposed on commanders and operations planners. "Ten" is an often-used allowable number and many operations are disapproved, if the expected number is higher.

Current practice can be contrasted with that in use on June 6, 1944. The Allied Air and Naval pre-landing bombardment of Normandy killed 3000 French civilians. Fully 20,000 would die before the Germans were pushed out of Normandy. The towns of Caen and St. Lo were flattened in the fighting right after D-Day. Further details on the history of French, Belgian and Dutch civilians killed on D-Day and the following weeks and months can be found in William I. Hitchcock's *The Bitter Road to Freedom* (ISBN 978-1-4391-2330-0).

It's an interesting contrast.

ABOUT THE AUTHOR:

William C. Grayson

Bill Grayson is formally trained as a USAF Intelligence Officer. He served as Commander and as Operations Officer of Air Force Signals Intelligence, Counterintelligence, and Operational Security units throughout Europe and Vietnam and served three tours at the National Security Agency as a Cryptologic Staff Officer and as the Chief of Transmission Security, overseeing all DoD joint service programs.

Following his USAF service, Bill joined the US Dept. of Commerce as a Telecommunications Specialist/Team Chief securing the computers and communications of whole federal agencies across the US and Latin America. He specialized in drug enforcement and maritime security.

Next Bill was a Senior Security Consultant with leading aerospace defense and Federally-Funded R&D Contractors in Washington. In that capacity, he was an Information Systems Security Architect of networked computers at NASA, Defense, Treasury, Justice, and Transportation Depts. and performed special activities for the White House, Air Force 1, the JCS, NATO, and the Nuclear Regulatory Commission. In support of Homeland Security, Bill supported Coast Guard Port Security studies on all three coasts and contributed to a White House plan for distributing intelligence among federal, state, local, and tribal jurisdictions. He is also an appointed member of his hometown's Public Safety Committee and a contributor to Maryland's School Emergency Planning Guidelines.

Bill holds BA and MS degrees and is a student of six foreign languages. He is a Certified Computer Security Professional, an Operational Security Certified Professional, and NSA COMSEC professional. He is a member of the AF Association, VFW, American Legion, Freedom Through Vigilance Assn, Military Officers Assn, NSA Phoenix Society, RAF Chicksands Alumni, and the Tan Son Nhut (Vietnam) Assn. He lives and works in the Maryland suburbs of Washington.

CPSIA information can be obtained
at www.ICGtesting.com
Printed in the USA
LVHW03s2232050618
579730LV00002B/4/P